M000104960

MEXICO WAY

MEXICO WAY

by Chilton Williamson, Jr.

Chronicles Press
Rockford, Illinois
2008

Copyright © 2008
All rights reserved. Printed in the United States of America.
No part of this book may be used or reproduced in any manner
whatsoever without written permission, except in the case of brief
quotations embodied in critical articles and reviews. Inquiries
should be addressed to The Rockford Institute, 928 North Main
Street, Rockford, Illinois 61103.

Library of Congress Cataloging-in-Publication Data

ISBN 978-0-9720616-8-1

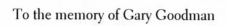

To the memory of Gary Goodman

Other Books by Chilton Williamson, Jr.

NARRATIVE NONFICTION
Saltbound: A Block Island Winter
Roughnecking It: Or, Life in the Overthrust
The Hundredth Meridian: Seasons and Travels in the New Old West

FICTION
Desert Light
The Homestead

MEXICO WAY

PART ONE

"I don't want to be married any longer."
"What does that mean?"
"What I said."
"You don't love me."
"I don't love anybody."
"You loved me. Or said you did."
"Nobody's responsible for what they said twenty-five years ago."
"I love you."
"I wish you wouldn't."
"Am I so tough to get along with?"
"Not tough."
"What then?"
"I think you are the most boring human being I've known ever, in my entire life. But that isn't the reason why I'm going to leave you."
"What is the reason?"
"I don't want to be married any longer."

Two weeks before his wife announced her intention to sue for divorce and ten days before she moved out leaving him the furniture, the toy poodle, her wedding dress, and several pairs of worn-out shoes at the back of the closet, Samuel Adams White, retired inspector with the United States Customs Bureau, had returned from a trip to Wyoming where he'd signed the closing papers on a forty-acre ranchette. The property, a yellow log house built twelve years before from a kit and surrounded by a buck-and-pole fence enclosing a sagebrush meadow stretching below stony peaks streaked with snow, was meant to realize a dream conceived by the inspector as a boy of fourteen when his father had taken him to see *The Virginian* at the moving-picture cinema in Spring Valley, in those days a dusty farm town of a few thousand people drowsing in the California sun fifteen miles east of San Diego. After quitting the realtor's office the inspector had walked down the main street where late-season skiers gawked before the false fronts of the frame buildings and entered a western-wear store, where he purchased blue jeans, three candy-striped shirts with yoked shoulders and pearly snap-buttons, a canvas duster that reached below his ankles when the buttoned hem was dropped, a pair of tooled boots with undershot heels, and a broad silver-belly hat with a curled brim and a silver ribbon circling the base of the crown. Next he'd driven in the rental car to visit the local horse-trader recommended by the realtor, with whom he left a one-thousand-dollar deposit on two quarter-horses and a pair of well-used roping saddles the trader happened to have on the place. The inspector was reconciled to writing off the horses, but hoped to rent out the property for the summer until he could make up his mind what he wanted to do with it in the long run. Wyoming, the ranch, horses—they belonged to the dream from which he'd awakened not to reality but into limbo. Faced by the destruction of the new life even before it commenced, the inspector had seized on the spectral form of the old one before it could evanesce. Back in Nogales now, he drifted like a ghost among scenes familiar to him from nearly thirty years of his professional and personal life, waiting to assume corporeal form among the flesh-and-blood shapes that jostled and sweated in the heat of the desert spring, although six weeks had passed already since his return to Arizona and Gloria's departure for California.

The turnstile spun silently in its barred cylinder as pedestrians passed back and forth between two sovereign nations, staring at the broken concrete pavement as if they'd dropped a dime or peso there. Once beyond the gate the Americans walked away briskly in the direction of the agencia de turista, while the Mexicans, losing their momentum rapidly, eddied against the high concrete wall where they stood watching their compatriots follow them through the turnstile. Beyond the auto checkpoint, traffic from Mexico was backed up under rusty palm trees as far as the bazaars where street vendors hawked rugs, leather goods, and trinkets in the sour-smelling calles between the drab grey buildings. On the plaza before a small gray church, two men with machetes on a stepladder hacked branches from a tree above the head of a Tarahumara woman squatted with her three children on the pavement as she attempted selling Chiclets to the tourists. Dirt streets descended precipitously among barrios strewn with garbage and prickly pear cactus on the two sides of the cañon forming a vent through which a southwesterly breeze carried the odor of mesquite fires, blending with a haze of leaded petrol fumes. Beyond the narrow pass in which the old town of Nogales, Sonora, stood, a vast metropolis of plywood and cardboard shacks, populated by several hundred thousand migrants and refugees arrived from the south in hope of entering the United States, spread itself over the plain that lay behind the hills. The inspector, after three decades, had never strayed beyond the twelve-mile limit past which the carta de turista was required of all foreigners, nor had he any intention of ever doing so. Marooned on the concrete island between opposing traffic flows, he held the poodle on a tight leash as a southbound station wagon, crowded with college students on spring break from the university in Tucson, eased by him. For thirty years the inspector had listened to the tales told by tourists returning ashen-faced from Mexico: hair-raising stories of ambushes by armed bandits, pursuing lorries filled with men

13

in anonymous fatigues and wielding automatic rifles, minor auto accidents resulting in the arrest of American citizens who were promptly thrown into prison and never heard from by their families again. He'd never been able to comprehend what reason or business Americans had to go traveling abroad in foreign countries, where history clung with pervasive tendrils like some poisonous tropical vine and where the God of nations still refused to show His face.

The dog strained forward from his knee, and the inspector stepped off the island and crossed among the cars halted in the southbound lane toward the loitering Mexicans who, as it seemed to him, gauged his approach with feral eyes. Familiarity had left him mostly indifferent to the Mexican people, but indifference in his case was not exactly neutrality. For the first time in many weeks the inspector was aware of himself as an object of human attention. Approaching the sidewalk he drew the poodle against his leg and for the next several blocks held her tight above the collar as they passed by the Mayoreo y Menudeo stores with their trays of cheap goods—flip-flops and tennis shoes and cowboy shirts and hats—obtruding onto the sidewalk to be picked over by Mexican nationals carrying stuffed shopping bags through a blare of Latin music. He took close hold again a block farther on as, beneath a retaining wall rising to the tall stuccoed church on the hill above the street, an Hispanic woman came toward them guided by a German shepherd in a leather harness. At the precise moment that she passed before the stone steps going up to the church the woman crossed herself, proceeding past the inspector with the blank, oblivious, otherworldly stare of the totally blind. As far as the end of the block he wondered how she'd known with such accuracy when she reached the church steps.

The walk was part of a daily routine by which he expected to reenter the familiar rut that would guide him unswervingly for the rest of his life, though at present, rather than walking, he felt himself to be floating above it all like a moonwalker. Around a curve in the street the inspector caught sight of the hotel, a wide building of white painted brick surrounded by palm trees and fronted by an expanse of tarmac crowded with expensive cars. Here tourists and retirees from the north joined the prosperous local business-men of the city who lunched daily in the restaurant and the lovely, leisured Latin women lingering in the cocktail lounge adjoining it. It was the inspector's custom to buy the morning paper in the lobby and read the news over breakfast in the air-conditioned dining room where, in spite of the many years he'd lived in Nogales, he knew hardly anyone to speak to beyond the retired import man who would repeat over and over the history of the produce business in Sonora and whose name the inspector was usually unable to recall.

After breakfast and the paper, the inspector returned to the rented bungalow (his house, already on the market, was confidently expected by the real-estate broker to sell within weeks) where he worked crossword puzzles and read until noon, when he took the dog for a briefer walk in the midday heat. He read the works of Zane Grey, Jack Schaefer, and Walter van Tilburn Clark, but Louis L'Amour's were his particular favorites. In these books the inspector recognized the America his father, a San Diego police officer, had taught him in his boyhood and in which he'd lost neither faith nor belief since: an America that won its battles, solved its problems, brought enlightenment and progress to the world, and had God on its side. By one o'clock the house, thick-walled and shaded by palm trees but equipped only with a swamp cooler, had become unpleasantly warm, and the inspector drove to a truck stop on the edge of town for lunch. Because Mexican or any kind of spicy food hurt his stomach, he invariably ordered a cheeseburger, french-fried potatoes, and a milkshake. After leaving the restaurant the inspector stopped by the supermarket for the few things he needed for his supper and a can of horse meat for the dog, and by three he was home again rereading Louis L'Amour, who being deceased was no longer writing books. At five he mixed and drank two gin and tonics, put a frozen dinner in the microwave oven, and ate his supper in the kitchen while doves called softly from the rooftops and wide Mexican women perambulated with their broods along the narrow sidewalk.

The house was fractured adobe covered by a tin roof on which the palm fronds clashed restlessly, fronted by a porch of warped planks at a second remove from the street above a concrete retaining wall surmounted by an iron fence and located in an old and seedy neighborhood inhabited mostly by Mexican and American hippies. In the second week of his occupancy the inspector had discovered a five-ounce packet of marijuana when he tripped and almost fell over a loose board in the hallway, but the deputy sent by the sheriff's department to take possession of the packet seemed unimpressed. The previous tenants, he explained, had been suspected of receiving smuggled drugs. However, the county lacked sufficient evidence on which to arrest them. The property was run-down and dirty enough that the inspector felt no shame for the lax housekeeping standards he'd allowed to replace a lifelong standard of cleanliness and military order.

Every evening after supper the inspector put the dog in the car and drove north on the interstate to an exit leading into a two-lane road that shortly became a dirt track climbing west into hills covered by Johnsongrass, live oak, and yucca and surmounted by red battlements of volcanic rock mottled with green lichen. Some miles beyond the pavement's end he stopped the car, let the dog out, and threw sticks for her to retrieve while he walked slowly in his new cowboy clothes over the thin grass growing among the cholla, watching the sun drop toward the steep black canyons cutting up from Mexico. They returned to the bungalow before dark, and the inspector, after locking the doors, securing the window fastenings, and changing into his dressing gown, worked another crossword and was in bed by ten o'clock. Since he'd neglected to have a telephone installed in the house, he was never disturbed by callers.

Returning from the hills somewhat later than usual one evening, the inspector spied through the dusk an indistinct figure on the sidewalk beside the iron gate, which he saw had been pushed partway open. He parked the car against the curb and stepped out, shutting the door against the dog who sat up on the front seat growling and showing her teeth through the windshield. The woman was small and dark, with a wide Mexican face. She wore a pale blue dress with a colorful Indian shawl over it.

"You are Señor Wilson?"

"No I'm not."

"You live here?"

"Yes."

Pinned by the car lights like a butterfly on velvet, she seemed confused. "Will the dog bite?" the woman asked.

"Not if I don't let her out of the car."

"I come twice now," she explained, "looking for Señor Wilson."

"He used to live here?"

"Yes, Señor."

"Then my guess is he's probably in jail." Watching her closely, the inspector thought he observed her mouth tighten at the corners as he spoke. "You had business with this fellow Wilson?"

"I am a fortune-teller," the woman said, and he could see her mind working rapidly behind her eyes. "For Señor Wilson only five dollar. For you also, five dollar."

"I don't believe in superstition."

"For the alcalde in Nogales, twenty-five dollar. I have many wealthy clients in México."

"You have much business on the American side also?"

"Oh very."

The inspector reluctantly extended his hand. "All right then."

The woman glanced nervously at the car, from which snarling sounds continued to come. "What about the dog?" she asked.

"She'll be okay until we're through."

17

"She is your special friend—yes?"

"I suppose she is."

"I will hurry," the woman promised, "so she will not be left alone for very long."

As she bent above his palm, the inspector looked over her head and up the street for the car he expected to see waiting in the darkness. "The lifeline is good," she said approvingly, "very deep and long. You have had a happy life already?"

"Average, I'd say."

"Your wife is no longer with you."

"We split the sheets last month."

"I do not understand."

"We were divorced in March."

"I am very sorry."

"I'm not."

"Perhaps you will meet somebody new in your travels."

"I don't like to travel." He wondered if she would suspect his motive if he suggested they continue the reading in the house.

"But you enjoy to travel in México, yes?"

"I've never been down there."

"Ah Señor, but you will go. Soon!"

"I doubt it."

"I see a trip," the woman insisted. "I see a long trip. México is very nice place for the Americans, señor. I am sure you will enjoy very, very much. There is very much to see in México."

"I don't have money to pay for a trip now."

"Is very cheap for the Americans to live in México—almost like you are our guest. Give your hand again, please, the reading is not over yet."

The inspector considered as she continued to pore over his hand, reciting her grave nonsense. Supposing that he found a pretext to detain her, on what ground would he be justified in summoning a law officer? Anyway he had no telephone. Though a pretty woman still, she had the worn look common to poor Mexican women past the age of twenty-five. He imagined her living in a shack of cardboard or sheet iron, warming herself and a large family at a mesquite fire and sleeping in a plastic bag on a hard dirt floor. The real mystery of her dark homeland was the ability of the human spirit to survive there at all—insofar as it *did* survive, he thought. The inspector felt relief as she finished the reading. He was retired now. What came and went across the border was no longer any business of his. He took five dollars from his wallet. The woman folded the bill into a tiny square and deposited it in a change purse she took from under her shawl. "Señor Wilson was your friend?" she inquired.

"He was not."

"So interested in the occult. A good customer of mine, very."

"I wouldn't be surprised if he was." The thought occurred to him that Wilson might have been purchasing something in addition to marijuana and fortune-telling. She was just pretty enough, and apparently competitive in her pricing.

"So many customers to see tonight," the woman told him, replacing the purse under her shawl. "Your friend, she cry for you. Muchas gracias, señor."

His interest dwindled with her receding figure as it blurred into darkness beyond the headlights' reach, but he watched it out of sight before returning to the car where he released the panting, yapping dog, which leaped from the seat and ran its leash out, jumping and twisting like a fish on the line. "Shut up, Darlene," the inspector said, and gave the chain a hard tug. "She isn't your worry, or mine either."

At age fifty-three the inspector was beginning to understand that what people call life is actually a sequence of lives, each separated by a small death after which the soul exists for a time in limbo before moving into and taking up the new life. How long this limbo lasted he had no idea. While hoping that it might end soon, he was unable to imagine the contours of the life to follow, as he felt incapable of summoning the energy to embrace it when it finally arrived. For the present lassitude wrapped him like a shroud in which, though hating it, he was nevertheless content to lie.

The heat was partly responsible, he believed. He'd never given a thought to temperature before, driving to work and back in an air-conditioned car, sitting all day in the manufactured blast of the cooling outlets. Now, though it was only the beginning of April, he was continuously aware of the white caloric glare of the sun emanating from a galvanized sky. When the swamp cooler broke down and the landlord was unable to get a repairman to fix it immediately, he began waking at five to read in the cool of the pre-dawn morning, napping through the midday, and lying awake until nearly midnight with the front door ajar on the latch and the windows open to thresh the cooling air passing stealthily in the darkness out of Mexico. Although he considered taking the house off the market and moving into it again, he gave up the idea for good after driving past the place one evening with the dog. The sight of the home he'd shared with his wife for thirty years gave him an appalling sensation of viewing his own mausoleum.

As the spring days lengthened in the premature heat, the inspector took to whistling up the dog at the conclusion of his siesta and heading immediately into the hills where he remained until evening and returned after dark, navigating the narrow trail with headlights set at high beam through clouds of flitting insects while the dog snapped at moths crawling on the inside of the car windows. Although more people were arriving to camp on the live-oak ridges and in the canopied creek bottoms, the little traffic on the road was mostly pickup trucks trailering bulls and saddle horses, ancient Mexican sedans bottoming out in the washes, and the pale-green four-wheel-drive vehicles of the Border Patrol looking to intercept mules backpacking their contraband through the steep canyons cutting north from Mexico. The patrol agents, well acquainted with the inspector, saluted him as they passed and often stopped to ask whether he had noticed anything suspicious along the road.

Headed for the freeway one afternoon the inspector stopped at the supermarket where, along with horsemeat, he bought a can of corned-beef hash, a loaf of bread, a pint bottle of whiskey, and matches. He hadn't camped since his days as a Boy Scout from which he'd learned little about the out-of-doors and forgotten most of that little, but this day the insufferable closeness of the adobe house spurred him to something like adventure. As a substitute for a tent and sleeping bag he carried an Army blanket to spread on the back seat of the car, and he recalled having seen much dry wood lying about under the live oaks. Somewhat intimidated by his own boldness, the inspector assured himself that if the night air grew intolerably chill he could be back safe in town again within the hour. And he had Darlene for protection.

The produce sheds at the north end of the city were silent, awaiting the midnight arrival of fruits and vegetables from Sonora in transit to the greengrocer markets of Tucson, Phoenix, and Flagstaff. Off in the hills feathered with mesquite and on the graveled alluvial fans spreading out from the mountains, vacation homes for snowbirds escaping the snows of Kansas City and Minneapolis were going up beside ranchettes owned by locals fleeing the crime and congestion of a Mexican-American border town. The inspector also felt the need to escape. He left the freeway and continued west through the low steepsided hills gripped by single-story ranch houses surrounded by satellite dishes, horse corrals, and power boats berthed on tow trailers and covered by a patina of the red desert soil. Shortly before the pavement ended he passed a turnoff to the man-made lake that, in thirty years, he'd never once visited, nor thought to.

The inspector drove for twenty minutes against the steep

21

beneath the sandstone battlements before he reached the familiar meadow, where he steered the car across hummocks of salt-grass and prickly pear to the edge of a live-oak stand. He let the dog out to run in circles with her nose to the ground and trailing her leash and brought out the supper things, which he placed carefully under the trees on a patch of bare ground. The afternoon heat had subsided, and already a light breeze flowed down from the broken pinnacles of rock. Keeping a close eye on the dog, the inspector gathered chunks of sandstone lying scattered around and placed them in a fire ring. Only after he'd begun to sweat from the effort did he realize he'd neglected to bring water and an ice cooler from town.

Yucca bloomed on the steep slopes, the pale clustered flowers exuding a sweet perfume from the tips of graceful stalks the height of a man, and higher. The inspector walked among them, dislodging rocks from the pressed beds that exactly fitted them and brushing the ants and cocoons from the undersides. When he'd gathered nearly enough rocks, he was out of breath and his hands were chafed and sore. Returning to a rock pile he had discovered, he bent and lifted a red flat slab. The deadly buzzing commenced as he began to raise the rock, and before his brain could signal his hands to drop it he'd uncovered the whole of the coiled snake colored a motley brownish color, with a forked black tongue and diamond yellow eyes. The inspector staggered backward clawing behind himself, tripped over another rock, and turned a reverse somersault in the grass. He felt himself already up and running as he untangled his limbs, looking back over his shoulder as if he feared the snake were pursuing him. He kept running, and Darlene came gamboling from another direction and followed him back to camp with the leg of a Coues deer in her mouth for him to toss.

They ate, he and the dog, as the sun, a fire encased in a globe of red glass, sank through the evening haze among the sinister bergs of Mexico and brightened the fortress of sandstone above them to the redness of blood. The inspector sat on the backseat of the car with the door open and his feet in the grass to eat while Darlene, tied to the trunk of a live oak, bolted horsemeat from the flat rock he'd set out for her for a plate. With the suddenness of a wall switch the sun shut off the lingering warmth and the desert cold struck, causing the inspector to reach for his jacket and pour himself a second drink. Perhaps, he thought, the blanket would not after all be sufficient until morning.

Night followed quickly. In the darkness the inspector could find nothing further to do. He satisfied himself that the fire was out, untied the dog, and signaled her onto the front seat. Under the dome light, he read Louis L'Amour until he developed a crick in his neck. Then he closed the book and went and urinated at a short distance from the car. Since before supper no traffic had passed on the road, and the stony wilderness around him was sunk in a profound gloom unrelieved by any human sound.

Somewhere an owl called and was answered by another and from the opposite side of the canyon a pack of coyotes broke into an insane cacophony of whoops and barks, causing the inspector to shiver beneath the thin blanket before, all at once, he fell asleep.

He awakened instantly and completely, almost in anticipation of the dog whose frantic barking he confused at first with that of the coyotes. The inspector threw off the blanket and lunged across the seat back for the glove compartment before recalling that he'd taken the pistol into the house to clean it several evenings ago, and forgotten to put it back. Now faces pressed dimly behind the window glass. They came at him from both sides of the car, and from the corner of his eye he saw the dog snatched up and her neck wrung like a chicken's. The blanket he had tossed away came back at him and slapped him across the face, wet and laden with a sweet overpowering smell that watered his eyes and agonized his nose and throat. For several moments he continued to struggle against the smell. Then, satisfied that danger had passed, he relaxed and succumbed gratefully to sleep again.

PART TWO

The inspector became aware by degrees of a bad taste, headache, and blindness. Darkness choked him with a foul smell, and his limbs felt wadded together like fish-worms in a can. It seemed to him he was being ungently rocked, the regular swaying motion interrupted by lurches forward and backward. When he attempted to lift his head from his chest a hardness pressed down on the crown of it and sent a stab of pain into his neck. Two hard round objects thrust upward beneath his chin. He tried moving his legs and discovered that the hard things were his knees. His hands had apparently been misplaced, but he found them after a search, fastened at the small of his back. Some coarse material was over his mouth and eyes, and by alternately gnawing at it and pushing it with his tongue he was able finally to work the stuff under his jaw. Using his nose as a finger he felt of the vertical place on which his left shoulder rested and encountered the roughness of unfinished wood.

His bewilderment was followed by the certainty that he was in his coffin under six feet of dirt, and the scream that rose in his throat only increased his terror: "*Aiiiiiiiiieeeeeeeeeeeeiiiwww!*" It was answered immediately by a second voice from the darkness, and then by a third. "Yawh," someone said contemptuously, to which someone else added, with a note of disgust, "Bleah!" Beneath this monosyllabic conversation the inspector perceived another sound: a series of rapid double-clicks spaced as in Morse code, a noise that he was in some way able to feel as well as hear. The stench, pungent and fetid, was nearly unbearable.

The inspector considered his predicament while sitting (or was he lying?) in his forced fetal position. At last he began to explore again with his nose the woody substance beside him until he discovered a surficial interruption and painfully, with immense effort, applied his left eye to it. As he did so a forward lurch caused his brow to strike painfully against the wood, the movement accompanied by a horn blast and the progressive clash of metal. "I am on a train," the inspector told himself. "I am in a wooden box on a train, probably in the baggage car." From the darkness the voices spoke again—"Yee-Aww!"; "Beh-eh-eh-eh-eh!"—and the full truth struck home. He had heard stories enough from tourists whose second-class tickets had entitled them to accommodations shared with pigs, chickens, goats, and calves. "I am on a train in Mexico," the inspector added. He felt like a doctor diagnosing himself as a cancer victim. In the same moment he was aware of the overwhelming desire to urinate.

The train resumed speed as roughly as it had slackened it. The inspector heard the bellow of the diesel engine and smelt the overheated brakes letting go. The car rocked between the rails as if it would tear them from the ties, and the horn blasted frequently for crossings. The inspector's headache worsened until his skull felt like hardened concrete and he was finally sick all over himself. In spite of his agony, or perhaps because of it, he fell asleep again and dreamed he was in a strange land populated by strange people and animals and overgrown with surrealistic trees and plants, garishly colored and outsized. When he awoke the train was halted, and pale light showed through the hole in the box. He put his eye to the hole and saw the night sky as an oblong of paler dark where the car door had been rolled back, and against it stars and lights being thrust forward and swung back and forth. The inspector heard orders given in Spanish, and sleepy oaths. Crates were offloaded from the car, followed by the mule and a procession of goats that showed in antic silhouette as they descended the ramp that had been set in place for them. His chin was wet with vomit and the stink of his box gave him the dry heaves, while his bladder had the rigidity of cast iron. The cloth like a cowboy bandana under his chin reminded the inspector that he could yell now, as well as see.

He watched as simian shapes with lanterns approached, but that single primitive cry of an hour (or two? or four?) ago had expended his vocal strength. The men laid hold of the crate and manhandled it across the floor of the boxcar, revolving it brutally on its corners so that his head banged crazily from one side to the other, and finally turning it upside down. The inspector fought to hold his water while attempting to determine whether these were his captors or innocent railroad employees. His head cleared as the chloroform subsided, permitting him to reassess the wisdom of crying out. Perhaps they believed they were disposing of a corpse, in which case the imperative was to play dead. "¡Vaya!" a voice exclaimed. "¡Qué hedor!" And another from outside the car, "¡Cuidado!" The inspector had no need of his limited professional knowledge of the Spanish language to understand that the aura surrounding his box had been noted and was being remarked on.

He was suddenly in free fall; the subsequent concussion to his head, knocked him nearly unconscious. An involuntary groan escaped him, followed by cries of surprise and alarm from the crowd. Heavy boots struck the ground as the workers vaulted down from the car, and the inspector observed with horror the play of searching lights through the crude breathholes bored at irregular intervals in the plywood. He had given himself away; the game was up now. They would pry away the top, tear him from the box like a child being ripped from its mother's womb, and finish the job on the spot. The railwaymen would care nothing, and do less.

Instead a silence ensued that seemed to the inspector to continue to the end of time, and past it. Finally he slid his cheek along the wood until his eye was once again aligned with the hole. The men stood grouped like actors in a play, splashed by lantern-light. As the inspector watched, a single figure detached itself from one of the groups and approached the man directly opposite him, holding his lantern high and his right hand extended. The man spoke softly so that the inspector was unable to hear his words, but the tightly folded wad of paper, illuminated by the kerosene flame as it changed hands, made hearing unnecessary.

The inspector withdrew his eye from the hole and held himself tightly as the box was lifted again and borne unsteadily through kerosene fumes and the press of men. He heard the sound of a tailgate going down and felt the slide of wood over steel as the box was jammed forward in the bed, but it was not until the engine fired roughly and the truck jolted forward in a reek of leaded petrol that his bladder gave way at last, bathing him in the reassuring warmth of his own wet.

31

The truck proceeded bumpily, its tires jarring now on one side and now on the other into deep potholes. The inspector, smelling mesquite smoke and hearing the blare of a cantina from the midnight silence, perceived that they were following the streets of a town. Presently he felt the vehicle swerve and make a sudden stop. Footsteps sounded above the idling motor, the tailgate came down with a crash, and boot leather scraped on steel as the men swung up into the bed and approached the box, one on either side. The top was ripped away and a hard light played down. "Se ha orinadó," a voice remarked with disgust. The inspector tried to raise his head, but they took him by the chin and gagged him once more with an oily cloth, above which they added a blindfold. They replaced the top of the box, jumped down, and climbed up laughing into the cab again. The truck lurched forward and picked up speed. A cold wind penetrated the box, chilling him in his dampened clothes, and after a time the inspector, in spite of his efforts to remain awake, lost consciousness for the third time that night.

He awakened slowly in the peace and security of childhood. Then the rooster crowed once more, and the inspector found himself still folded into his box and, as it seemed to him, near death from cold. The last time he recalled hearing a rooster was in his early adolescence when neighbors kept chickens and a milk cow behind the house and sold freshly picked tomatoes from a plank table in the street, before the developers who added a nearby subdivision had bribed the town councilmen to alter the zoning regulations to prohibit the keeping of cows and chickens. The inspector's back pained him terribly, his hands were partly numb, and he had no feeling at all in his legs and feet. The truck stood motionless, or perhaps he was no longer in the truck. Though the blindfold remained tightly in place the inspector, hearing the rooster crow once more, seemed to feel the darkness being drawn from the night sky by the happy cry of the bird. A breeze whispering about the box carried the odor of wood smoke, and he heard the slap of a screen door, followed by the fall of boots striding purposefully over hard ground.

They dropped the gate again, and one of the two men climbed up by the rear bumper. The aroma of sweated clothes and sour, unbathed flesh stifled the inspector as the men grappled bear-like with the box, wrestling it onto the gate from which he, after teetering for an instant like a man in a barrel going over a falls, toppled sickeningly. "¡Ay cabrón!" a voice swore above him. The inspector felt the box jerk, then level abruptly as a boot toe was removed from beneath it.

The man in the bed jumped down, and the inspector tilted back as if in an airplane taking off. The sensation was followed by a soft pneumatic flow similar to the flight of a light aircraft. Fear having given way to a preoccupation with sightless physical perception, the inspector's mind hesitated only briefly on the edge of an assured leap: He was riding on a dolly, being wheeled rapidly over slightly uneven ground. The rooster crowed again above the scratch and flutter of other barnyard fowl, and then the inspector heard the voice of a woman, hushed but not far away. It seemed to him an oddly familiar voice, but his interest was eclipsed entirely by the cooking smells—odors so blissfully compelling that tears started in his eyes, and the inspector was forced to bite his tongue to keep from crying out.

He felt the harder bump of the dolly crossing a threshold, followed by the whispery sound of the tires in some soft substance. The inspector was jolted forward as the men righted the dolly, and felt the shudder as they drew it from under the box. A pause ensued in which the inspector imagined his captors staring above folded arms, as if curious themselves to learn what would follow next. The rank human smell closed about him once more as the men began to strike with blunt and heavy instruments at the wooden walls of his prison.

When the box finally gave the inspector gave with it, falling head first onto coarse reeking straw. Someone stepped forward and tore the oily cloth from his mouth and the blindfold from his eyes. He felt the material pull away and wondered why he still saw nothing, before he realized that his eyes were screwed shut like

33

those of a child expecting a blow. He tried to move but, finding himself unable, lay where he was with his knees under his chin and his hands behind his back until he was raised, not ungently, from behind to a kind of frozen crouch while someone thrust a chair beneath him. The chair had a straight high back, and when they let go of him he fell forward on his face again into the straw and they had to pick him up and set him upright on it once more, his back molded in a paralytic curve by the box. At last they brought a length of rope and tied him into the chair by the wrists and shoulders. The pain was excruciating, and twice he could not prevent himself from groaning, but they paid him no mind. Until now he'd been able to visualize the scene in imagination and only when they had ceased pummeling, tugging, and pulling at his limbs did his eyes finally open, without his willing them to do so. The inspector looked. And nearly fainted from fear.

He who had never been a religious man understood that, whether heaven existed or not, hell was the most terrible reality. A single kerosene lantern set on the straw partially illuminated a grotto formed of crumbling adobe brick roofed by ocotillo poles lashed with wire against an evil red sky that glowed in the broken places. Beyond the circle of light, hideous misshapen heads with glinting yellow eyes hung suspended in the looming shadow, and a chain of rusted heavy links was attached to the opposite wall beside a torn and stained mattress with the springs protruding from it. As the inspector stared upon these things in horror, the men moved out from behind the chair and stood facing him with their hands in their pockets, staring back.

There were three of them, he saw to his surprise. Two were obviously Mexicans, one tall and strongly built, the other shortish and stocky, both looking to be in their forties. The taller man wore a sombrero, and a sarape thrown over his shoulders; the shorter, a battered straw hat and long black mustaches that added ferocity to his comically round face. Both had on western shirts, blue jeans, and cowboy boots. Their companion was not yet a man, thin and underdeveloped with the smooth dusky skin of an Indian. The boy, who wore his black hair long like an American hippie, had crooked yellow teeth and a slight harelip; he was dressed in a

U.S. Army jacket over a T-shirt on which the message WE ARE THE OVERLORDS was printed, jeans, and a pair of new American-made jogging shoes. The short Mexican scowled beneath the jammed-down hat, the brim of which came nearly to his eyes, but the other man, chewing through his beard on a wooden toothpick, looked merely contemptuous. The Indian boy drew a package of chewing gum from the pocket of the Army jacket, unwrapped all five sticks, and shoved them into his mouth at once. When at last the short one spoke, he did so quietly, in an even voice. "Do you know who we are?" he asked, in English.

The inspector wanted to answer but his tongue lay dry in his mouth like a dead fish. He shook his head. No.

"Look harder, man."

Again the inspector shook his head. No. No.

The Indian boy blew a bubble the size of his head. He burst it and prodded the expended sack back into his mouth with the tip of a pale prehensile tongue.

"Piense. Think."

The inspector continued to say nothing, and this time he did not even move.

The man turned to the boy whose face was again eclipsed by a pink elastic globe. "Anda a llamar a María."

The boy disappeared at once ahead of the diminished smack of the bubble in the open air. The silence that followed was broken eventually by the stamp of a hoof and an impatient exclamation, "Yaaaaaaaaaaaawh!"

"¡Cállate!" the short man ordered sharply, "Benito Juárez!"

Presently they heard footsteps approaching the structure, and the Indian boy entered, ducking his head below the rough plank lintel. He was followed by a woman, small, rather pretty, and wearing a pale blue dress with a colorful Indian shawl over it. "Bueno," the short Mexican said, taking her by the arm and turning her to face the inspector. "You know her?" he added, almost in a conversational tone.

The inspector looked. To him, Mexicans—even the women—had always been indistinguishable from one another. Then he looked again.

"You know her?"

The inspector's chin wobbled. "The fortune-teller," he croaked.

"Sí, la adivina. She knows you too. María has a good memory. She remembered."

The inspector looked again at the woman, who turned her face aside and covered it with her hand. "Está bien," the man said, "estoy seguro. You are the man. Ándale, María. Tenemos mucha hambre."

She left without looking at any one of them, and the inspector heard her running light-footedly away across the clear pink light of morning. "Now we give you to drink," the short Mexican said, "and cover up your mouth again afterward."

They gave him stale-tasting water, one holding his chin back while the other poured directly into his mouth from the dented canteen. Then they dragged him between them through the straw to the mattress, attached the chain to his ankle, and retied his wrists. Finally they put the gag in place again. "María will send food with Alberto," the man promised, "when he comes to feed the mules."

Alone in the early twilight, the inspector lay on his back on the ruined mattress, listening to their booted feet striding rapidly away together. Unexpectedly the rooster crowed again, and this time the sound gave him no joy or even comfort, but instead filled his heart with despair.

He was fed by the woman María and guarded and exercised by the bearded man who never appeared without the sarape and sombrero and whom María called Pancho. Pancho was always careful in removing the ropes from his burned skin and with patience supported him in his shuffling turns around the shed each morning and evening, but the inspector sensed hostility and contempt behind the silence that remained unbroken save when the Mexican gave him an order or inquired tersely about the tightness of his bonds and whether he wanted a drink of water from the tin bucket standing against the wall by the door. Pancho removed the blind and the gag when he came in the morning, and replaced them at night when he carried the kerosene lantern away. When on the first day the inspector ventured to ask the reason for his abduction, Pancho had looked through him as if he had not heard the question. He repeated it that evening while María was feeding him broth from a wooden spoon and Pancho had stepped outside to urinate, but she had replied only by placing a finger to her mouth and shaking her head so vigorously that she spilt the hot soup down the front of his shirt.

Also on the first day Pancho had stripped away the Wyoming cowboy clothes, grimey with a paste of dirt and oil and stiff with dried urine, from which the inspector's wallet and small change had already been removed along with his wristwatch, and with these the hand-tooled sharkskin boots. In their place he brought a rough flannel shirt and a pair of loose cotton pants belted by a length of rope in which he dressed the inspector before carrying the boots away by the finger straps. He had come again at nightfall with a blanket to cover him as he lay on the mattress with the exposed springs gyring into his back, but the thin covering was insufficient to prevent the inspector from waking stiff with cold before morning, his stomach clenched from shivering as he heard the slow stamp of the mules and sleepy flutter and cluck of roosting chickens. Shortly after daybreak, María arrived accompanied by Pancho and carrying a plastic bucket that contained his breakfast: two sugar-sprinkled pastries filled with sour apples and a large tamale that tasted wonderful to the inspector but afterward gave him heartburn and made the terrible diarrhea he'd developed painful as well as humiliating and exhausting. She brought him coffee too, and when they had gone the inspector savored the last of it as it cooled in the battered tin cup they allowed him. The temperature rose steadily inside the shed where the chickens already sought refuge from the blinding heat beyond the door, scratching holes in the dry dirt against the wall for their dustbaths. In the morning after Pancho and María had left him, the Indian boy came and turned out the mules and the goats, and at evening brought them to the shed again. In this way the inspector passed several days.

He could not watch the sun cross the sky from east to west, but through the broken roof he saw its incandescence and felt the heat at midday like the steady exhalation of a behemoth silently watching over him. Were it not for the sun, whose habits he had never troubled himself to observe before, the inspector might have imagined that time was standing still for him now, in his captivity at the hands of desperadoes in the heart of darkest Mexico. While it was not lost on him that he was among the wretchedest of men—those whose worst nightmares have suddenly become reality—he was astonished to discover that the realization not only was without terror, but accompanied by a suspension of will and emotion that seemed very like peace. Years before, standing at the bedside of a mortally ill relative, he'd heard the man whisper, "I must be dying, it isn't as bad as I thought," and been shocked by his words. Now, the inspector thought, he knew precisely what the old man had felt.

On the afternoon of the third day of his imprisonment, as he lay drifting in a kind of half-sleep on the torturous mattress, he was roused abruptly by a loud flutter and the hysterical cackle of a chicken. The inspector raised his head and, staring among the growing shadows, discerned a cloud of dust against the wall and at the center of it a pair of white wings beating above a twisting muscular shape, grayish brown in color and of approximately the thick-

38

ness of his own leg. As he watched, the thing rose and swayed in hypnotic rhythm, oblivious to the blows it received, and suddenly the inspector shouted. He shouted and bellowed as if the terror were writhing inside him, eating at his heart and liver and spleen, and within moments heard boots pounding toward the shed, followed by Pancho's face in the wooden frame of the door. "¿Qué te passa?" Pancho demanded harshly. "What's the matter with you?"

The inspector raised himself to a sitting position against the wall to which he'd rolled and pointed a shaking finger toward the corner of the shed. "Snake," he gasped, feeling the sweat burning on his eyelids. "It ate a chicken."

"Culebra," Pancho agreed with him. "México tiene muchas culebras. And many chickens too."

"It could have crawled in my bed!"

"Only on a cold night."

"The nights are always cold here!"

Grudgingly Pancho considered. At last he said, "I will stretch a lariat around the bed, when I come with María tonight."

"A lariat!"

"Of course, a lariat. No snake will cross a rope of any kind."

"Can't you find a cot—something to lift me up off of the ground?"

"There is no such thing around. A lariat is all that is necessary."

"Good God, man! What are you keeping me here for anyway?"

"You will know soon enough. I promise you."

"I have no family. My wife divorced me last month. Nobody knows where I am, or cares. There is no one to pay ransom for me."

"No one is interested in money."

The inspector sat up and extended his bound wrists in crippled supplication. "For God's sake, let me make a phone call—a single phone call is all I ask. I will ask my broker in Phoenix to send you as much money as you wish."

Pancho on his way to the door turned on his heel to face the captive. He had removed the sarape today in acknowledgment of

39

the heat, but under the brim of the black sombrero his eyes were bright and angry. (The inspector noted, for the first time and with something of a shock, that they were blue eyes.) Presently the Mexican spat, deliberately and with extreme contempt, into the straw, and even then he did not speak at once. Finally he said, "You gringos think that you can buy everything: luck and love, happiness and health; honor. But you, amigo, are about to learn something that would make you, in your own country, a wise man, and that is that you not only cannot buy honor but that you cannot always buy dishonor, either. Buenas tardes. If you see another culebra before I bring the lariat, take care not to look him in the eye, lest he hypnotize you."

That night María fed him a thick mutton stew with hominy and bits of sheep bone in it, while Pancho scuffed dry straw over the damp messes the inspector, from incontinence, had made around the mattress. When he had eaten, María took the plate and spoon and cup away, and Pancho retied the gag and blindfold and bound his wrists once more. With the blindfold in place, the inspector no longer lay awake struggling against helplessness and the absolute impenetrable darkness but lapsed almost immediately into sleep. This evening he had not slept very long when rough hands seized him and shook him roughly awake. The men did not speak, but the inspector had no trouble recognizing Pancho's quick impatient breath and the labored asthmatic breathing of the other one. Without waiting for him to get control of his legs, they jerked him to a standing position between them and thrust him forward. "¡Anda!" the voice of Pancho commanded. The inspector walked.

They walked him out of the shed and across the moonlit yard where the night breeze carried the odor of cactus flowers and his stiff toes curled to grip the hard-packed soil through his sock feet to the house, which was warm and full of the unventilated smells of mutton stew and boiled coffee. The inspector heard around him the stifled cry of cats and a muffled plaintive corrido on the radio, turned low. The men moved just behind and ahead of him, maintaining their grip as he stumbled over a tall threshold, and then another. He was conscious of doors opening at their approach and of the familiar household sounds receding, and then the three of them halted abruptly and stood linked together for several moments like spelunkers before they jostled him forward again, but more slowly. "Cuidado," Pancho urged him, "desciende. Step down."

Step by step between them, he felt his way down wooden stairs that creaked beneath his weight while a subterranean coolness rose around him and closed finally over his head. The boards were rough and splintered, and sudden ground underfoot told him they had finished the descent. The short man, stepping heavily off the stairs at his back, collided with the inspector and bumped him forward against Pancho, who cursed under his breath and swung him about by the arm. Together they marched him several paces, and halted again. "Sit down," Pancho ordered, and the inspector lowered himself tentatively onto a chair that wobbled slightly on the uneven floor. "We will be back in a while," Pancho added. "Do not think of going anywhere until then." Their boots rang out on the stairs, and the inspector heard the trapdoor being reset in place overhead.

The chill was like the touch of the darkness entombing him as the inspector sat rigid in the chair, his senses straining to detect the slightest sensation. He heard occasional steps passing above, and once he felt a rapid movement across his foot. The inspector, kicking out with the foot, contacted some warm soft thing that squeaked sharply in pain and surprise as it scuttled on across the dirt. He did not move a muscle after that, and presently the steps returned above him and the trapdoor was lifted again. The murmurous voices and the sound of gathering feet alerted the inspector to the presence of several people. Slowly they descended the stairs and moved out around him, as the trap came down with a soft bump. The inspector felt the fan of air as bodies passed back and forth and smelt the smell of burning candle wax, mixed with a more pungent and fragrant odor barely familiar to him. Then hands were at work untying the knot at the back of his head, and the low voice of Pancho was at his ear. "Do not be afraid," Pancho encouraged him. "There are four people here, who you already know. And one other."

When the blindfold was taken from his eyes he had to shut them against the brilliance of the candles that blazed out at him like fireworks from the surrounding dark. He kept them shut until the pain had ceased and, opening them, was astonished to find himself in church confronting a man-sized plaster figure surrounded by candles burning in tall colored glasses. The figure wore a robe of deep purple over white underclothes and long black hair parted above a high brow, and the inspector, in spite of the dusky unfamiliar complexion of the statue, had no trouble recognizing it

42

as an image of Jesus Christ. Behind the figure portions of a wall of fitted stone, illuminated by the candles, stood forward from the darkness, and candles placed against the side walls revealed grottoes at a level of five or six feet above the floor inset with smaller indistinct figures. Three people—the short man, the Indian boy, and María—sat to the left of the Christ statue on chairs taken from a cheap aluminum kitchen set, by which the inspector was assured that the hand that gripped his shoulder from behind was the hand of Pancho. The man and the boy were staring at him, but María looked at her lap. They stared a long time before Pancho, after clearing his throat, spoke: "En el Nombre del Padre, y del Hijo, y del Espíritu Santo—comencemos."

It had been such a trivial affair, the inspector had put it easily out of his mind, though that was not exactly the same thing as forgetting about it. Three-and-a-half months before, he had confiscated contraband transported by a Mexican truck at the Port of Entry after uncovering from beneath a load of melons many hundreds of wristwatch knockoffs bearing the names Cartier, Rolex, Tiffany, and Patek Philippe. Several days after this routine seizure, the inspector was changing the car oil when a Mexican approached him in the driveway and presented a bogus Cartier watch for sale. The man endured a lecture on the evils of smuggling and afterward replaced the watch in his pocket. Then, calmly, he offered a payment of five thousand dollars cash to allow a truckload of watches across the border the following week. Later the inspector was convinced that it had been the venue, not the substance, of temptation that accomplished his fall. The pact had been sealed with an oily handshake on the sun-warmed apron of his own garage, a neighborly arrangement arrived at under the upraised hood of an automobile in the clear white light of an Arizona winter day. While five thousand dollars was small potatoes to an official who had been offered hundreds of thousands in bribes in the course of a career lasting thirty years, it happened by chance to be exactly the amount the inspector needed to complete the down payment on the contracted ranch in Wyoming he was at that moment preparing to close on. He was able to send the balance north by Federal Express within the week, and on Tuesday of the

43

next, at eight o'clock in the morning, was at his post to watch for the produce truck bearing the Sonoran plate number he'd written into his pocket notebook. It arrived nearly three hours late, well within the ambit of Mexican punctuality but at an hour when the traffic north was inconveniently heavy. However, the driver had identified the correct booth, and the inspector stepped out and looked the truck over, lifting melons one by one and shaking them conscientiously beside his ear. If only he had been less conscientious, having crawled on hands and knees beneath the chassis, he would not have gone on to have a look into the tool box, where twenty kilos of marijuana packaged in clear plastic lay stashed. In retrospect, the inspector was uncertain whether his subsequent action was spurred by integrity or simple loss of nerve. He held up the load and had the driver arrested. Later, the watches were found and taken from their crates beneath a couple of tons of green cantaloupes.

Pancho, in recounting the story, faced directly toward the statue as if he were addressing it, tall and straight and hatless with the sombrero trailing from his hand. He spoke first in Spanish, before repeating in English what he had just said for the benefit of the inspector. His voice, though impassioned, was devoid of anger, and he interrupted the narrative at intervals to elicit confirmation from the short man and María. Throughout his address he never removed his gaze from the plaster face, yet to the inspector it seemed that the painted eyes were fixed not on Pancho but rather upon himself. Though Pancho kept his back toward him, it was as if he were using the figure as a ventriloquist's dummy and a medium to communicate indirectly with the prisoner. The eyes were at once stern and sorrowful, loving and judging, and they told the inspector everything that he would ever need to know about himself. In an attempt to avoid them, he forced his own gaze sideways and tried to concentrate on the strange recessed figures in the walls which his focusing vision recognized as dried and shriveled homunculi the color of mahogany wood, the eyes sunken, the lips drawn back from the long ivory teeth, the genitals hanging like pencil stubs between the bowed and wasted thighs.

When the inspector's turn came to speak he did not comprehend what was expected of him and had to be prompted by Pancho, who gripped him tightly by the upper arm and lifted him out of his seat. Three times he started to speak, each time in English, and after the third attempt ceased for good. It was no use, he knew: Everyone present understood as well as he, or better, the nature of his offense and the measure of his guilt, which were beyond all defense. He would not be forgiven because the essence of justice precludes forgiveness and mercy, as gravity forbids a weighted body from flying upwards. It did not matter if the judge were the best and the fairest man in the world, since it was precisely his goodness and fairness that demanded justice inexorably. From the corner of his eye the inspector saw María bent forward from her seat, as if in prayer.

The inspector did not raise his eyes when the verdict, "Culpable," was spoken. Afterward he welcomed the blindfold that hid them all from his sight, and him from theirs.

He was awakened the next morning by Pancho who had come in place of María with his breakfast, stringy beef stewed with red chili peppers and warm tortillas wrapped in a torn but clean dish towel. The inspector was surprised to discover that he had a good appetite for the food, though the chili was like a fiery sword thrust down his throat into his belly. While the Indian boy turned the mules out, Pancho felt in the straw along the wall until he had his hands full of chicken eggs to which bits of feather, down, and shit adhered. "Pretty fresh," Pancho said. "María will make a fine omelet tonight."

"So I am guilty," the inspector said. "What are they going to do with me now?"

Pancho knelt and arranged the eggs carefully on the tin plate the captive had wiped clean with the last scrap of tortilla. "¿Castigo?" he asked. "Punishment?"

"Yes."

"Gringos," Pancho said in disgust. "Always wanting to know what is going to happen to them before it happens. You think you can prevent what is going to happen to *you*? That is not the way for any man living in this world. Yesterday morning you asked me what are you being kept here for. Today you know the answer to that question. Tomorrow, the next day, someday soon, you will know the answer to this one, too. ¿Más cafe?"

He had brought a large ironware pot instead of the smaller china one María carried; its greater volume held the heat better, so that the inspector for the first time in his captivity had hot coffee to drink with his breakfast. This gave him strength and, he discovered, courage from an unsuspected reserve. Pancho, rising from his knees, lost balance as he lifted the pot and spilled coffee from the spout over the sleeve of his shirt. He set the pot down in the straw with an oath and rolled back the sleeve to the elbow, exposing a sinewy brown forearm marked with a blue-and-red tattoo. Pancho drew a bandana handkerchief from the back pocket of his jeans and rubbed vigorously at the arm with it before turning down the sleeve again. "You were in the American Air Force?" the inspector asked, before he could think.

"I was." Pancho waited a long time before saying it.

"But—you are a Mexican citizen!"

"I was born," Pancho said in a careless voice that suggested candor was of no importance now, "in Great Falls, Montana. I am called Pancho Villa Gillespie, Jr." He added proudly, "I chose the first two names when I became a citizen of Mexico."

"But you're an American!"

"Not me," Pancho told him. "Not Pancho Villa Gillespie. I hate America, and I hate Americans. All Americans."

"But how can you treat me, a fellow American, this way?"

"Easy," Pancho said.

The inspector felt that he was going to be sick to his stomach. He had never in his life, he thought, imagined such complete treachery, such utter villainy. "How long were you in the Air Force?" he managed to ask.

"Thirty-eight months, twenty-seven days. I went AWOL when I was on R&R in Guadalajara in 1968, after I learned they was sending me for another tour in Vietnam. I have never set foot in the United States since that day." He added after a moment's reflection, "Except to pick you up."

That evening when the Indian brought the animals into the shed a rattlesnake waking after the heat of the day bit one of the mules over the cannon bone on the off front leg. The mule screamed like a woman and reared up, shattering the roof of ocotillo poles with its head. As the other mules whirled and broke for the daylight, the inspector saw the boy leap forward with a piece of plank in his hand and strike three times with it at the snake's head. After the third strike he threw away the plank and raised the limp body behind the evil wedge-shaped skull from the straw. The snake was between five and six feet long, as thick at the middle as a ship's hawser. The boy carried it to the door of the shed and threw it off into the cactus. Then he went for the mule and led the animal, trembling and rolling its eyes, to a wooden post in the yard. He snubbed it there and commenced running his hands over its body, addressing it with comforting words as if it were a human person. Already the leg had swelled until it was almost the thickness of the post. The boy stroked the black shoulder, ran his hand down the leg, and lifted the hoof by the fetlock. He inspected the leg carefully before setting the hoof down, and then the inspector, from a sitting position on the mattress, saw him take a knife from the leather scabbard on his belt and make two quick cuts in the hide, to which the mule offered no objection. Then he replaced the knife and, kneeling, applied his mouth to the bright blood flow. He sucked at the wound, removed his bloody face from the leg, spat a crimson stream onto the ground between the planted hoofs, and reapplied his mouth to the cut. He did this several times before rising and going on to the house for a bowl of water and a handful of rags which he used to wash the swollen leg and bind it. By now the swelling had mounted as high as the shoulder, but with gentle words the boy was able to coax the mule on three legs to the shed, where he covered it with a threadbare blanket and fed it a measure of grain from a coffee can. When he had finished with the mule, he went out and drove the others inside with it again. Finally he retrieved the snake from the cactus and nailed it through the middle with a spike to the top of the post: a grisly hieroglyphic for the inspector to ponder until the darkness, rising out of the desert hard pan, hid it from his sight.

It was María who waked him as she undid the gag and blindfold in the light of the kerosene lantern. She had come alone he saw, bringing with her a bottle of tequila half consumed above the curled worm resting at the bottom of it. "Beba," María urged him; "tome una copa." She tipped the bottle and set the mouth of it against his lower teeth.

The inspector hesitated before drinking; he was still half asleep, and he loathed tequila. Reluctantly he sipped, and was instantly aware of a radiant warmth spreading throughout his body. Though he had become accustomed enough to the cold of the desert night that it no longer disturbed his sleep, once roused he felt its chill like a second skin beneath his clothing. María tipped the bottle again, and he sucked greedily at the reservoir of golden liqueur. "Beba," she said again. "I would not blame you to get drunk tonight."

48

Stiffness prevented the inspector from rising, and María placed an arm about his shoulders to help him into a sitting position. "I am sorry now," she said. "It was a sin for me to tell my husband how I see you in Nogales. You are angry with me—yes?"

"I want more tequila," the inspector said.

She gave him more. "Now Jesús is going to kill you, and I will go to Hell. Until then I will pray for you. And afterward you are dead I will pray for you every day, and have a Mass said for you on that day every year and at Christmas. You will no go to Hell, because you have killed nobody."

"I don't think he will kill me. I will give him the five-thousand dollars back."

But she shook her head. "You do not understand. You are an American. This is México."

"My country will not let him get away with it. They will extradite him and sentence *him* to death."

"But they will never find him. He will be with the growers in the Sierra Madre, where even our own Federales are afraid to go."

The inspector had no heart, in spite of the tequila, to bluff any further. In a voice that he tried unsuccessfully to keep from shaking, he asked, "When is he going to kill me?"

"Tomorrow we are going into the mountains to visit the growers. It is two days' journey by car. You will be with us when we leave here, but not when we arrive there. In the mountains."

The inspector felt his bowels, ravaged by the great Montezuma, beginning to move again. He reached for the bottle, and María, cradling him in her arms like an infant, tenderly presented it to his searching mouth. "I am sorry," she said, "but it cannot be helped now. Please pray for me to the Blessed Mother when you are in Heaven. Pray that, when I too die, her Beloved Son will not send me to burn forever with all the sinners in Hell."

María returned before the sun was up, with cold coffee and the warmed-over remains of the stew whose ingredients had fused indistinguishably in a blackish lumpy paste. As if in apology for the meal, she called his attention to the sweetened condensed milk she had added to the coffee. "It is impossible to cook this morning," she excused herself. "There is no firewood, and Jesús will not let me bring more—he say we must hurry now."

A pale glow showed along the hem of the night sky, like footlights coming up on the final act of a play. The tin cup was cold in the inspector's cold-stiffened hands, and abruptly a pack of coyotes broke into a demented overture from the gravel hills above the rancho. The inspector shivered. "¿Estás frio?" María asked.

"Yes, I'm cold," the inspector told her sharply.

"Jesús put the last of the tequila into his coffee last night. But in a little while it will be warm."

"Warm? Christ, it'll be hot enough to fry eggs."

"In the car it will not be so hot."

In the car, he thought. Going where? The coyotes, continuing their savage uproar, were answered by another pack far off in the hills.

"Do you fear?" María asked.

"No," the inspector said. The truth was, he was unable to believe that today he was going to die, incapable of believing his own death.

"I fear," María said. "Nine good First Fridays will not make up for what I have done. My mother told me that Jesús was a bad man. I should not have married Jesús. But I am his wife. ¿Comprende?"

"No."

María sighed. "I am very sad," she said.

"I know how you feel."

They heard the stamp of boots outside the shed as the men arrived: the expatriate, Jesús, and the Indian boy, Alberto. Alberto still wore the military jacket and jogging shoes, but he had exchanged the bubble gum for a cigarette that made him look somewhat older, and much more sinister.

Pancho untied the rope from his ankles, cursing the stench from his filthy trousers, and when María had gone he and Jesús undressed the inspector and bathed him with water from the water bucket. Chilled still by the night air, it burned his flesh and made his bones ache, and he was grateful for the ungentle rubbing-down they gave him with the sweat-stiffened horse blanket Alberto borrowed from the stricken mule, who the boy said was not doing well. "Malo, muy malo," he told Jesús in a morose voice. Then they dressed him again in a clean pair of cotton pants and rebuttoned his shirt, and Jesús and the expatriate walked him up and down in the straw until he was able to take a few steps by himself. From the back of the shed they could all hear Alberto speaking pleadingly to the mule as he spread hay around with a pitchfork. Finally Pancho retied his wrists and ankles, loosely, and stuffed the gag and blindfold into the back pocket of his own pants. "Listo," he told Jesús when the man returned from the stalls where he had been inspecting the mule. "Trae el carro aquí."

Jesús, shaking his head, looked exasperated. "¡Ay cabrón!" he exclaimed, "Momento," and faced back to the stalls again. "¡Dispara!" Jesús shouted to Alberto. "¡Dispara ya!" Then he went out to get the car.

It was a Chrysler sedan, more than twenty years old and painted a sun-faded red, wide as a boat and squatted low on ruined springs. Strips of vinyl fluttered from its shredded landau roof on the dawn breeze, and a staccato jet of exhaust accompanying the rough idle of an engine missing on several cylinders was barely visible in the gray light. Jesús sat behind the wheel with an AK-47 automatic rifle beside him, María on the back seat holding a picnic basket. Behind the car the eastern mountains showed flat black against a sky ascending in bars of yellow and orange into the cobalt blue of unchased night.

Pancho shoved the inspector toward the car, where he paused to light a cigarette. Then he opened the door and pushed him inside, while María moved over on the seat behind Jesús. When

51

the inspector was settled in the middle of the seat the expatriate climbed in beside him, and Jesús blew the horn. He waited a minute and blew it again. A loud report sounded from back of the shed, and almost immediately Alberto came running toward the car holding a large revolver in his hand and jumped into the front seat with Jesús and the AK-47. "Gracias," Jesús said, taking the revolver from him and stowing it with the rifle beneath the seat.

As the Chrysler swung around in the yard a stand of saguaros on a hill above them wheeled like a company of soldiers against the lightening sky. Wholly preoccupied by despair or self-pity, the inspector was unaware until they had already reached the paved highway that the guttural noise from the front of the car was the sound of the Indian boy Alberto, crying.

The sun's rim appeared over a stony lip of the range, and golden light flooded the valley where they traveled eastward. The valley, easing south like a wide green river between two ranges of brown sugarloaf hills, was divided by a spring torrent of muddy water overflowing the cottonwood groves and stripped automobiles along its banks. Cattle grazed behind strands of slack wire supporting crooked posts hacked from the surrounding mesquite trees, and a pair of bay horses stood placidly outside the fence in the right-of-way beside the road, their front feet hobbled by strips of torn bedsheet. All the car windows were rolled down, letting in a sweeping breeze mixed with a thick road dust and the smoke of Jesús's and the expatriate's cigarettes. Now and then the inspector glanced furtively at María, but each time she was staring with apparent intensity at the passing countryside while drumming with her fingers on the top of the picnic basket.

They crossed a dry gulch half filled with bottles and cans and the rusting shells of overturned automobiles, and came to a village of cracked adobe houses and cratered dirt streets where chickens scratched and small children on bicycles towed skateboards behind them. The TECATE signs were switched on at this early hour in the grimy windows of the cantinas, and beggars slept late or loafed in the shade of the drooping green trees. The car overtook mule-drawn wagons and farm trucks loaded with hay and entire families crowded in the cab, before it was delayed at the rail line by a train made up of two baggage cars and three coaches crawling past the gate arm as a woman and her three children waved impassively from the curtained doorway of a boxcar shunted onto a disconnected rail spur. When the train had passed, the arm remained in the horizontal position until a man at the front of the line stepped out of his pickup truck and raised it by hand. Jesús drove across the single track and along the calle mayor, past a simple white church surrounded by severely pruned trees and worshipers coming from daily Mass. At the intersection beyond the church, he ran an ALTO sign. "¡Ay!" Alberto exclaimed. "¿No has visto al guardia?"

The guardia had been standing by his machine in an alley partially obscured by false orange trees. Hearing the sudden roar of a motorcycle engine behind him, Jesús swore under his breath, and María snatched a rosary from her pocket and said a prayer. As the Chrysler swerved against the curb and slowed, Pancho leaned toward the inspector and said in a casual voice, "One word from you, and you're both dead. Muertos. Difuntos. ¿Comprenden?"

The guardia braced his machine behind the Chrysler and walked up to the driver's window, from which Jesús's elbow remained nonchalantly thrust. Jesús showed no awareness of his presence until he was spoken to. Then he handed up his license without looking at the man or turning his body in the seat. The guardia examined the license carefully, then bent to the window and looked from one of the passengers to the next. He let his gaze rest for a time on the inspector who stared back, unable to tell whether his face expressed everything or nothing. "Y él," the guardia said finally to Jesús. "¿Quién es?"

Jesús shrugged. "Mi amigo. De Estados Unidos."

The carta de turista, the inspector thought suddenly; please let him ask to see my carta de turista.

A loud pop sounded from the front seat where Alberto had exploded an enormous bubble of gum. The guardia's torso snapped back, and his hand dropped to his holstered gun. Then his body went slack, and his face grew red. "¡Indio sucio! Con respeto, por favor." But at the sight of the rolled parti-colored bill Jesús extended negligently through the window, the guardia appeared mollified. Deftly, with an unobtrusive pass of his hand like a magician, he palmed the bill and returned without a word to the motorcycle. "¡Gracias, gracias, O Santa Madre!" María cried softly, returning the rosary to her pocket as the powerful engine gunned behind them.

As the guardia shot past the Chrysler and canted sharply into the next street, the inspector recalled the stories he had heard of the brutalities of Mexican policemen and wished he had been privileged to experience a few of them.

When Jesús had driven several miles from town he pulled over against the borrow pit and went back and lifted the trunk of the Chrysler, from which he brought automatic pistols for himself and Alberto and the expatriate. Then he drove on again.

The day had become a blinding glare, tremulous with rippling heat waves in which distant trees and cacti wavered like weeds in a gentle current, and the wind through the open windows of the car was a dry and searing blast. Having left the valley at its eastern perimeter, they were following a gravel road into the foothills of the taller mountains, traversing steep ravines in which filaments of muddy snowmelt ran. The saguaro lay below them now, and the grassy ridges were covered with spaced manzanita, delicate umbrellas of feathery acid-green leaves over black-barked frames, and sprays of ocotillo whose gray thorny poles sprouted spring leaves and scarlet terminal flowers like a heron's opened beak. Shadows of hawks sailed across the road, and a thousand feet above turkey vultures circled on ragged black wings against the cyanic sky, craning their red rubbery necks in search of the dead and the dying. Two of the vultures had alighted upon a whiteface cow lying on her back at a short distance from the road with her four legs standing stiff as posts around her grotesquely distended belly. One bird stood perched on her head from which it had already removed the eyes, and another straddled the pelvis, tearing the rotting flesh from a gaping wound where a mass of grayish maggots seethed. As the Chrysler drew abreast the carcass, Alberto leveled his automatic pistol, thrust it through the window, and fired a shot into the drumtight paunch, which exploded with a sound audible even above the engine and collapsed in a cloud of poisonous flatulence. María cried out and covered her face with her handkerchief, and the inspector just avoided being sick in his hands.

As they ascended higher by the switchbacks, the valley they had left narrowed to a green belt scratched by white lines connecting the farmhouses with villages that glittered dully like heaps of broken glass under the glaze of the westering sun. The inspector looked down upon the green canopy of the mesquite forests, and up at the platoons of spanish bayonet marching steeply downhill to the road through fleshy agaves and the perfumed white-blossoming century plants and yucca. Cattle grazed along the creek beds in the long ravines, fattening on the spring grasses, and once Jesús had to pull onto the swag of a curve to make way for a battered ranch pickup with a stock rack slid into the bed and carrying two saddled horses. The driver, who wore a red bandana under his chin and a dusty black hat drawn over his eyes, did not acknowledge them as he pressed by. A flowery dust covered the vegetation along the road and dragged behind the car, reversing itself with the wind on the switchbacks to overtake them in choking white gusts that caused the men to swear and roll the windows up. They were climbing now to the live oak and alligator juniper zone, and the inspector was shocked to observe the similarity between this cañon and the one from which he had been abducted. It had never occurred to him that any part of Mexico could resemble the United States.

Wedged into the angle between the seatback and the door, María slept with the picnic basket at her feet while Alberto, his boot heels propped on the dashboard and the bill of his cap pulled down to his nose, appeared to doze. The expatriate, though he had released his hold on the inspector's arm, still gripped the pistol in his lap. The inspector kept his eyes fixed on the red turrets of rock lifting around them, and once he turned in the seat to gaze back at the valley through widening spools of dust. "Why do you hate America?" he suddenly asked the expatriate.

Pancho looked at him with vacant astonishment, as if he had forgot entirely about the inspector and never heard of the United States. But as he began to speak, the look hardened.

"I flew bombing missions over North Vietnam," Pancho began. "At orders from the Commander in Chief in Washington, Lyndon Baines Johnson, I killed hundreds of innocent men, women, and children, destroyed hundreds of square kilometers of forests, ruined thousands of hectares of farmland. I married a Vietnamese

56

woman and had a son by her. Both were killed by what the Americans called 'friendly' fire. My buddy was captured by the Cong and tortured to death after being locked in a tiger cage for two years. I believe I am now developing cancers from the Agent Orange I loaded into my plane. But that is not why I hate America." He paused to watch two men who looked like Indians going on foot with bedrolls strapped to their backs and leather bota bags slung over their shoulders. The men were smeared with a paste compounded of dust and sweat, shirtless, and wearing worn-out huaraches on their feet. They walked with their heads down as the Chrysler approached, and they did not look up as it passed them. "Why then?" the inspector asked.

When the expatriate turned again, his face was distorted by a fierce contempt. "I hate America," he said, "because of what America has become. A country of make-believe, where the people do not live with reality anymore, do not even know what reality is. America began as a Third World country, like Mexico. Today it is an empire of dumb rich people. I think that when America was a Third World country, it was the best country. Now I know that it is the worst. And that is why, amigo, I hate *your* country."

The road narrowed as the slope steepened on both sides until it was scarcely more than a shelf carved from the face of a red cliff rising almost vertically overhead and descending less drastically through squared boulders and talus fallen from above. Here the sharpened curves were blind ones. Jesús slowed the Chrysler to horse speed and hugged the wall on the passenger side. Eastward across an abyss of crystalline space the true mountains rose, ridge upon ridge of blue, their tilted snowfields glinting from the highest ranges. Barely in time to avoid collision, Jesús jammed the brake pedal as the nose of a white Jeep station wagon pushed cautiously around the cliff and, seeing them, stopped abruptly. Almost at once the Jeep began easing forward again, and the inspector was able to make out six pale faces inside, three couples, all of them drawn and scared looking. They were young faces, nearly childlike and of a startling innocence. The Jeep carried Arizona tags, and as it drew up beside them the inspector recognized the familiar university T-shirts and the din of American rock music. The driver put his hand out the window to indicate that he wished Jesús to stop, and the Chrysler came to an obedient halt. Inside the Jeep, the music was instantly modulated. "Excuse me," the young man said, pronouncing his words exaggeratedly and spacing them widely. "Can you tell me if this road goes to Benjamin Hill?" He gave the name its English, rather than Spanish, pronunciation.

Jesús stared at him. Then he shrugged his shoulders indolently. "No hablo inglés," he explained

Looking distressed, the driver turned to the girl beside him and said something to her. She was a pretty blonde with a cigarette in her hand. The cigarette was hand-rolled, and a thermal slipping along the rock face carried to the inspector's nose a whiff of its cloying, pungent, unmistakable scent. Dropping the hand to her knee, the girl leaned across her boyfriend's lap and addressed Jesús. "¿Es el camino por Benyameeneel?" she asked in college Spanish and a sugary tone, like one speaking to a child, or a puppy.

Jesús did not answer her at once. Alberto, who had removed his feet from the dash and pushed back his cap, regarded the Americans without expression while the expatriate, his white-knuckled hand tight around the automatic pistol, sat rigidly straight. "Sí," Jesús said at last.

The six Americans relaxed and favored him with wide smiles evenly set with orthodontically perfected teeth. "¡Gracias, muchas gracias, señor!" the blonde said, as the inspector, watching her lovely face, felt overwhelmed by love for her, and for the rest of his own kind. "¡Muchas gracias, señor!" the driver parroted, lifting his foot from the brake. The Jeep slipped forward, all six pink and white faces beaming and bowing like Mandarins. It had passed the Chrysler by no more than a single length when the inspector shouted. In the instant, the expatriate had his hand over the inspector's mouth and the pistol barrel in his ribs. The Jeep's brake lights went on; the vehicle stopped, hesitated, and moved slowly in reverse until it was again alongside the Chrysler. The driver's face was puzzled, and a little concerned. "You guys want something?" he asked. Jesús looked at Alberto. "Tira," he said simply.

The blast of the AK-47 within the passenger compartment of

58

the Chrysler was excruciating. The driver's head unfolded like a fleshy pink and red flower in the first spray of bullets, and the girl was flung backward against the passenger door, her white T-shirt decorated by an embroidery of scarlet stitchwork. As the Jeep began to roll forward on the slight incline, Alberto jumped from the Chrysler and opened fire again across the Landau roof, drawing left to right in a single exquisitely smooth gesture like the stroke of a samurai sword. The young man in the middle seat collapsed into the lap of his girlfriend who, pinned beneath her lover's weight, was unable to move; Alberto caught her with the return sweep, nearly cutting her in two. The couple in the jump seat, partially shielded by the spare tire, were wounded but not seriously hurt. They wrenched the back door open on the off side of the car and jumped from the Jeep as it began to pick up speed, and Alberto drilled the girl between the shoulder blades. Blue blood sprayed from the bullet holes, and she turned several somersaults down the road after the car as Alberto fixed the rifle on the young man, severing his legs below the hips. The Jeep careened off the road and over the cliff, its tape deck blaring across the sudden silence of the stony wilderness, turned gracefully end over end, and exploded in a ball of orange flame against a house-sized boulder where it burned with controlled intensity beneath rolling balls of black smoke ascending to a perfect sky. Alberto kicked what remained of the final corpse after it. Then he checked the banana clip on the rifle and got back in the Chrysler beside Jesús. "Turistas," he said, grinning broadly. "Gringos."

The grip on the inspector's arm relaxed as the muzzle of Pancho's gun withdrew from behind his ear. "Hollywood don't make 'em any better'n that," the expatriate said, grinning broadly. "Do they?"

They ate a picnic lunch by a sandstone pool of desert water below a miniature fall, inset in a grassy bank blooming with baby's breath and surrounded by piñon pines offering shade and protection to the Coues deer and the brilliantly hued small birds that came flocking to the spring.

Alberto lugged the hamper to the largest tree and set it down on the waxy needles in the shade, while Pancho pulled the inspector from the car and Jesús, walking off a few paces and turning his back on them, relieved himself against a rock. The expatriate was careful to retie the inspector's hands before pushing him ahead to the tree, where María was spreading the clean white cloth she had taken from the hamper. She had brought freshly made enchiladas, a salad of sliced red and green peppers, tomatoes, and onions dressed with vinegar and oil, goat's cheese, and bread. Everyone drank with cupped hands from the pool except the inspector, whom Pancho offered the stale water remaining in the canteen to drink before thrusting the open neck beneath the waterfall until it overflowed. Fat gray and white jays scolded and swooped upon them from the piñon trees while they ate, and when they had finished Alberto went for the AK-47 and gave it a thorough cleaning. Jesús and Alberto ate well but María little, and the inspector did not eat at all.

They drove on across broken rimrock fractured by the grasping roots of the piñon and juniper forest and split by cañons choked with brush and boulders. From time to time the mountains toward which they proceeded appeared through the dark little trees as banded shades of green surmounted by the shining snowfields, no nearer-seeming to look at but more like mountains nevertheless. The winds blew cooler over the mesa, and toward the middle of the afternoon they saw below them a narrow valley of saltgrass and yucca, drained by a stream running between slender cottonwoods and bisected by the single track of the road they were following. As the Chrysler descended laboriously to the valley they could hear above the grind of first gear the roar of the creek, running much higher than had been apparent from the mesa. Jesús pressed the car to the stream's edge and stood with his boot toes almost in the current and his fingers thrust into the back pockets of his jeans, staring at the surging water. "Ay cabrón," he said. "Mierda." Nothing remained of the bridge but two nearly submerged piles of stones restrained by chicken wire on opposite sides of the creek. "¡Qué puñetera suerte!" Jesús protested.

Alberto left the car and went and stood beside him, also to stare at the creek. Pancho ostentatiously slid open the breach of his pistol to expose the brass casing of a shell. He handed the weapon to María, while giving the inspector a significant look. "Que no se le ocurra," he warned. "Women make better shots than men." Then he too got out of the car and stood with the others by the flood. For some minutes they watched the brown water rolling down its burden of silt and sand, before Jesús said something to Pancho across the Indian between them and Pancho after a pause answered in the same way. Jesús lifted his shoulders and spread his hands from his sides as if to say, "Then what else?"

Jesús spoke rapidly to María through the rolled-down window as the expatriate and Alberto began lifting tools from the trunk of the Chrysler. These they threw down on the bank. Afterward Pancho returned to the car and gestured at María and the inspector to come out of it and sit on a cottonwood log beside the creek. He showed her how to hold the gun, and warned the inspector again to do as the woman told him. Then he got behind the wheel of the Chrysler and drove it up cañon several hundred yards to a fall of rock, while Jesús and Alberto set to work with an axe and handsaw felling cottonwood trees.

They chopped broad wedges in the white tree meat, and narrow ones from the opposite side of the trunks. When they had three trees down, Pancho returned with a load of rock in the bellied-down Chrysler, and Jesús sent Alberto to help unload the rocks and carry them to the creek. Braced in rushing water to their knees they had set the first rock in place by the time Jesús had felled six trees. Alberto rejoined him when Pancho took the car up cañon again. The inspector, looking toward María, saw that

61

her face was gray and strained and that she appeared to have aged fifteen years in the past three or four days. To his surprise and also fear, he found he had lost track of the days of his captivity.

Pancho arrived with a second load of rock, and Alberto left off axing once more to carry and place the stones in the river. When Alberto and Pancho had worked together for some time in the creek with their pant legs rolled above their knees, balancing their weight against the solid onrush of water, the Indian boy took the expatriate by the sleeve and pointed, grinning, in the inspector's direction. Pancho nodded, waded from the creek, and went over to the log where María kept the inspector covered with Pancho's gun. "¡Qué venga!" Pancho told her. To the captive he said, "We'll see now how well she has been feeding you. Those who eat must work for their food. And remember, she still has the gun."

Pancho untied the ropes from the inspector's ankles and wrists and ordered him to turn the legs of his cotton pants to his thighs and remove the woolen socks. Then he led him to the creek bank and gave him a sharp push toward the water and toward Alberto, standing soaked to the waist and reaching to take hold of the inspector's hand. Alberto was chewing gum again, and he was still grinning.

The cold felt like steel wire sawing at his shins midway between ankle and knee. The inspector gasped, but the hand of Pancho between his shoulder blades pushed him forward. He looked down at his feet, pale and oversized and wavering in the roiled water, and took a step ahead of himself. The pain of the rocks on his tender soles was intolerable. He cried out and sank, writhing, to his knees and felt the terrible cold move farther up his legs. Behind him, Pancho laughed. "Hacia adelante," he urged. "Otro paso más . . . Otro más . . . Otro . . . Okay. Alto."

The inspector staggered to brace himself against the swift current while Pancho brought rocks from the car and hurled them down upon the building causeway for him and Alberto to work into place. After twice being almost swept away, he discovered that he was most secure when facing upstream at a forty-five-degree angle with the upstream foot planted ahead of the other. His torso was wetted by the splash of the rocks, and his legs became rapidly

numbed and without feeling as he labored side by side with the
Indian boy, who sang a corrido lustily around his wadded gum.
Like an automaton, Pancho walked back and forth between the car
and the creek, pressing the rocks against his abdomen and throw-
ing them farther and farther out as the causeway proceeded toward
the middle of the stream. Jesús by now had finished cutting trees
and sat resting himself on one of the silver stumps, surrounded by
piles of white chips and branches, their leaves already withering,
lopped from the straight long trunks. The sun stood low above the
back wall of the cañon, and the shadows of the remaining cottonwoods at the ford stretched far along the bank when Jesús, rising
from the stump, shouted to Pancho, and the expatriate, after depos-
iting the last load of rock, gestured at Alberto and the inspector to
come out of the creek. In his hurry to comply, the inspector stumbled and fell in the water whereupon Alberto, from behind him,
ducked his head and held it playfully under the wavelets until he
felt his lungs would explode. He emerged choking and sputtering
from his baptism and grabbed the extended hand of the expatriate
who drew him, stumbling on blue legs and feet, up to the safety of
the bank where the inspector stripped away the wet clothes and
wrapped a blanket about his violently shaking body.

When the men reached camp, María had a fire burning and a
coffee pot and Dutch oven set beside it. As soon as she saw the
inspector—blanketed, barelegged, and barefooted—she took his
clothes from Pancho and hung them on a pole near the flames.
The inspector had failed to notice the cow camp from the creek.
The house, built of the local sandstone rock, was an unchinked
one-room affair, so low-roofed that Jesús had to stoop when he
entered through the plank-framed door. Behind the house were a
ramada covered by piñon and juniper branches and a metal cistern
half-filled with brackish water and algae. The inspector saw no
cattle, but two horses, left behind by gauchos moving their cows
toward the mountains away from the summer heat of the desert,
grazed upcañon at a short distance from the camp. The horses
were of no use to Jesús, who promptly appropriated a pair of hand-
worked roping saddles and their blankets left behind in the stone
house. These he stowed in the trunk of the Chrysler with the tools

63

and assorted paraphernalia.

Pancho waited for the inspector to knead the blood toward the extremities and allowed him time for the shaking to subside before he bound his feet and hands once more. Then at María's request he went in search of firewood, while Jesús added oil to the Chrysler's engine and Alberto, taking his pistol, wandered away from camp past the horses. A succession of flat snapping sounds ensued, and presently Alberto returned carrying a handful of songbirds and four squirrels by the tails. Sitting crosslegged on the ground he skinned and plucked these, and dropped the small corpses into the Dutch oven to which María added a copious amount of Crisco. From the pine forest above them an owl called and was answered by another owl and then a third one far away, while cliff swallows dived against a fuchsia sky. They ate with their fingers as the flames deepened from yellow to orange in the fading light, and the inspector, who had expected his stomach to rebel at the prospect of squirrel, finished all that was given him and a whole jay as well. He was content to be warm, dressed in dry clothes, and well fed after an afternoon of excruciating physical labor. María poured coffee for him afterward and the heated liquid in his belly made him sleepy, so that he dozed off and fell face forward almost into the fire.

The inspector awoke on the back seat of the Chrysler with his feet hanging through the open door and a blanket over him. From habit he looked at his wrist and then at the moon which stood at the zenith, poised to begin its descent. With difficulty he raised himself on one elbow and saw that the fire had subsided to a glimmering heat beneath a crust of charcoal, and that beyond the fire moonlight filled the cañon like a gas. Snores sounded from the rock house, and then the inspector heard once more the noise that had wakened him: a woman's voice, soft and very close at hand. "¡Despierte!" María urged him. "¡O, despierte, señor!"

When she had worked the rope free of his ankles, María climbed onto the front seat and reached across the back of it to release his wrists as well. "¡Dese prisa! Es tarde ya. You must go now—inmediatamente!" Seizing his hands in her two small ones, she jerked the inspector to a sitting position. "¡Afuera!" María insisted.

He climbed painfully from the car and hobbled on stiff sore legs behind the woman, who finally reached behind herself to take his hand. Together they moved down cañon away from the stone house, María putting a finger to her lips each time his woolen feet snapped a stick or turned a pebble. "¡Silencio!" she warned. "The Indian has the ears of a hawk." When they were out of sight and hearing of the house, she led him more rapidly toward a grove of juniper trees pointing sharp as iron in the silver light. As they approached the trees a dim shape behind them stirred. The inspector flinched. "Es el caballo," María reassured him. "Only the horse."

As his eyes accustomed themselves to the shadow, he recognized one of the gauchos' horses under saddle and snubbed to a tree limb. "My husband would have killed you yesterday along with those other Americanos," María said, "but Pancho's idea is to give you an early start and kill you later."

The inspector, who no longer required urging, was about to

put his foot into the stirrup she held for him when he paused instead. "What will they do to you when they discover you have let me escape?"

"Better to die now and be in Heaven than live to be an old woman and go to Hell. But they will not suspect me, señor. It was I who told them where to find you, en primer lugar."

The inspector hesitated, but only for an instant. He who had not been astride a horse since he had taken abbreviated riding lessons at a boys' camp in the state of Washington in the summer of 1963 leaped for the saddle and was halted only by the woman's hand on his arm. María turned the stirrup for him and placed a hand under his thigh as he grabbed at the horn. Then he was mounted and looking down at her face, which was divided in hemispheres of light and shadow. "Ride straight down the cañon," María advised him, "and do not take the horse above a walk. I have blindfolded the other." As he turned the animal's head, she added, "Please pray for me, señor. Adiós."

As much in fear of the beast beneath him as he was of pursuit, the inspector did not look back at her as he rode away, lurching and swaying like a sack of flour tied upright in the saddle, under the tiring moon.

The horse found the trail at once and kept to it against the cañon wall at some distance from the creek, dropping into dry washes and following old braids in the floodplain before it rose again to the clay bottom overgrown with greasewood and cholla beneath a vast architecture of rock inset with hanging gardens and luminous in the moonshine. When he had ridden what he estimated at half a mile, the inspector cautiously let out rein and the horse immediately picked up its feet and broke to a faster gait. In his attempt to remain in the saddle he lost control of the bit, and the horse increased its pace to a lope which terrified the inspector before he discovered to his astonishment that the faster gait was easier to sit. Gripping the reins and the horn tightly with both hands, he forced his buttocks against the cantle and leaned forward in the saddle, letting the horse find its own way through the uproar of shod hooves ringing out from the verticalities of rock around him.

He could not have said how long they continued in this way before the horse slowed back into its terrible jolting trot and finally to a walk. The inspector was aware only that by then the cañon floor was in absolute darkness, while the moonlight, in striking the opposite wall at a declining angle, drew long shadows from the turrets of rock and penetrated the eerie caves and grottos beneath them. He felt a prickle along his spine and wished to urge the horse to a lope again, but feared to tire it. The walls on both sides of the cañon were much lower now, and they had moved considerably farther apart.

Gradually the inspector became aware of a vague source of light replacing that of the dying moon, as well as of an accompanying cold that intensified until he could hardly feel his feet in the stirrups and his hands around the horn. Dawn found him stiff and exhausted, without food or matches, leading the horse between sharp gravel hills where fans of ocotillo sprang in the gray light among a thin forest of mesquite trees. The inspector, for reassurance, turned to look back at the large and tired animal plodding behind him. It was a bay gelding with a black mane and tail and a white blaze that overran the fleshy part of its nose, swaybacked and ganted but nevertheless well muscled and sturdy. Its toes were badly grown out, and the off rear hoof from which the shoe had been cast left a distinctive print in the dust of the trail. The inspector glanced at the sky but read no particular time from it. By now the kidnappers would have awakened and discovered him missing. He found some comfort in the thought that while there were three of them, only one horse remained at the camp.

The train of cottonwoods bordering the creek swung eastward from the cañon's mouth, and the trail followed beside it at a remove of several hundred yards toward the thin bloody stain on the horizon. A pair of leather bags was strapped to the saddle immediately behind the cantle. The inspector opened one and found two waxed paper packets, each of which held a large bean tortilla, stale and beginning to mold. He wrapped the tortillas up again and replaced them in the bag, and went around the horse and opened the other bag. In it was a leather bota half-filled with bad-smelling water. He put the bota back in the bag too and hesitated by the horse as he tried to recall from which side he was expected to remount. Finally he decided on the right and swung up clumsily as the horse moved out, achieving a trot before he was sufficiently settled to take its head. Balancing himself with the reins as well as the saddlehorn, the inspector endured the trot in the knowledge that his pursuers would be traveling faster than he and from the necessity of taking the greatest possible advantage of the lead María had given him. The stain in the eastern sky ahead of them continued to spread and brighten, and a cold breeze arising out of nowhere pierced his cotton pants and shirt and the bootless woolen socks that slipped forward through the stirrups as he rode. When the liquid sun bounced above the mountain front and began its ascent through wheeling spokes of light, the inspector tucked his chin into his chest and permitted the horse to break to a lope, riding with a loose rein and without bothering to guide it as it followed the familiar trail away from the cañon.

A shuddering behemoth shriek rose suddenly from between his knees and the inspector, nearly unhorsed, lifted his head and saw between the pricked ears that they were bearing down at a high rate of speed upon a corral where a group of horses stood resting their chins on the top rail to observe their approach. The bay whinnied again, and was answered this time by one of the corralled horses, and then by another. A long adobe house stretched beyond the corral and also more corrals, and barns, and lemon and cypress trees, fixed and imminent in the spreading light. Pivots in sections stretching many hundreds of yards flung loops of silver water across fields as green and flat as billiard tables, and the sun's early rays, feeling within the open door of a tractor barn, touched upon gleaming green-and-yellow metallic shapes while caressing the svelte contours of a sports car of European make parked on the curved drive before the house. Almost weeping from relief and gratitude, the inspector slipped down from the horse and held it with difficulty by the reins as it pranced forward to greet its fellows. The shutters were closed over the windows of the house, but from somewhere close by he heard a man's voice raised in exclamation. Thoughtlessly the inspector dropped the reins and stared around, while the horse trotted to the corral and touched noses in turn with the other horses along the rail. The cry came again, and the inspector was about to answer when it was replied to by a child's excited laughter from behind the screen of oleander in purple flower stretching between the corrals and the adobe house. Forgetful of the horse, the inspector crept to the bushes and peered through them.

A tall, very slender, and extremely handsome young man stood at the center of an oval of yellow sand enclosed by a low white-washed wall, pushing a two-wheeled cart with a set of ox horns attached to it at a small boy of seven or eight who stood with planted feet flapping a red cloth about himself as the cart passed. Each time the boy flapped the cloth the man, nodding vigorously, shouted, "¡Olé!" and the boy, beaming, responded with a burst of laughter. After three or four passes the horns caught the scarlet cloth, whereupon the child screamed as if in terror and the man shoved the horns and cloth together into his chest, crying as he did so, "¡Corneado! Estás muerto!" He stood holding the cart by the handles as the boy gingerly pulled the cloth from the horns with a sheepish expression.

The inspector was about to push ahead through the bushes when a dim recollection from childhood stopped him from doing so. The riding instructor at the boys' camp had explained that horses were magnetically oriented animals. If you became lost on horseback, he had said, you needed only to give the horse his head and he would find the way home for you. Even if they did not believe that he had stolen the horse, the kidnappers when they caught up with him at the ranch would assure them otherwise, and he would either be turned over to the Mexican police or remanded to the custody of Pancho and Jesús. Attempting a backward step, he found himself rooted like a tree when suddenly the child screamed, "¡Papá! ¡Papá! ¡El Diablo! ¡Mira! ¡Mira! ¡Papá!" and pointed his finger directly at the inspector's face glaring like a demon's from the oleander.

The inspector backed out of the bushes like a buffalo and tore across the grass in the direction of the corrals. It occurred to him as he ran that the horse might have wandered away and deserted him, but he found it standing quite still, trailing its reins as it touched noses with a big Appaloosa gelding. The inspector was mounted in an instant with his sockfeet securely in the stirrups as he turned the horse's head from the rail and thumped its flanks with his heels. The animal made a leap and came down running and they went at a gallop across the cacti and creosote bush in the direction of the great riverine cottonwoods. They plunged through the treeline and slid down the clay bank into the coffee-colored river that surged around them bearing tree branches and bark and gobbets of yellow foam. The horse swam strongly, cleaving the freshet with its thick neck, its legs striving mightily in a kind of gigantic dog paddle, and they made the opposite bank no more than a hundred yards downstream from where they had entered the creek. The bank was steeper on the far side, and the horse beat with its hooves and thrashed against it, covering the inspector's soaked clothes with the greasy mud and nearly going over backward into the rushing water before it found foothold and scrambled up to the grassy verge. The inspector checked it only long enough to recover the stirrups and take a good hold on the horn before they went on at a gallop again across the desert, steaming under the glaring sun like a wayward locomotive.

The desert was a cruel implacable enemy of the personal variety that had first surrounded him, cutting off every avenue of escape, and next conjured the sun to train its focused rays upon him as if he were a bug tortured by an evil child amusing itself with a magnifying lens.

He was on foot again leading the exhausted horse, his filthy clothes dried to the stiffness of cardboard, the woolen socks holed and bloody. Somewhere the horse had dropped another shoe for their pursuers to find, and already the grown-out toe had broken off and been worn even with the flat of the hoof by the stony outcrops that emerged from the hardpan. Twice the inspector, with a yelp of pain, had dropped the reins to stand on one foot while he drew the spines of prickly pear cactus from the other, and several times the teddybear cholla had struck at him like a snake as he passed and injected its barbed quills into his arm.

They were crossing a desert plain whose rough texture—palo verde, creosote bush, mesquite, saguaro—softened as it receded toward the distant mountains until it acquired the appearance of green velvet. East and west of the plain, ranges of naked brown rock turned a harsh pink in the terrible relentless light, and behind the eastern ridges taller mountains rose up, capped by shining snowfields. These mountains were familiar to the inspector, who was able to recognize them as those toward which the smugglers had been traveling. From this he concluded that he was presently on a northern heading for the U.S. border.

The desert floor was carved by dry gullies, and everywhere the carcasses of giant saguaro lay split open from roots to tip, their desiccated tubular plumbing exposed to the sun, as though they had perished from the heat and from thirst. Three times the inspector halted, took the bota from the saddlebag, and made as if to drink from it before he put it away again. The fourth time he unscrewed the top and, without sniffing first, pointed the bota directly down his gullet. The water tasted even worse than it smelled, and the inspector needed to brace himself to avoid regurgitating the stuff. He wanted desperately to lie down and rest, but the rock piles that offered the only shelter from the sun looked snaky, so he continued past them. At last when he felt he could go no farther, he espied by chance a large piece of lava rock and a smaller one beside it. The inspector investigated and discovered a low palisade of ocotillo poles fencing the flat ground between the rocks in which a small fire pit had been dug. He tied the horse by the reins to a small saguaro close by. Then he unfastened the saddlebags from the cantle and carried them to the enclosure, where he threw them down for a pillow and stretched himself on the firm cool earth. He was asleep even before he could stretch his legs out, dreaming that he was in flight on horseback across the relentless desert barely ahead of his pursuers who cried out to him with encouraging words, begging him to stop and wait for them.

When he woke it was late afternoon. The inspector lifted his head from the leather bags, withdrew one of the tortillas, and nibbled it around the moldy places. When he had eaten he drank several sips of the foul-tasting water and afterward went in search of the horse. It was nowhere to be seen, and he was unable to discover even where he had tied it until he came upon the little saguaro pulled from the ground by its roots and lying on its side on the hardpan surrounded by fresh hoofprints and horse manure. The inspector followed the tracks into a stony fissure where, beneath a live oak tree standing against the rock wall, the horse stood drinking at a spring bubbling from the sandy soil imprinted with the delicate tracks of birds and rodents, the dragging ones of lizards, and the rippling signature of the desert sidewinder.

He left the horse tied to the oak tree while he went back for the bota, which he emptied into the firepit in the enclosure before returning to the spring where, after getting down on all fours to drink, he refilled it with the sweet cold water. Then he led the horse out of the rock cleft, replaced the bota in the saddlebags, and retied the bags into the saddle strings. Finally he mounted, wincing at the pain to his torn, aching, scorched, and weary feet, and rode forward to the top of a low rise where he halted once more and sat the horse like a cavalry officer, shading his eyes with his hand as he surveyed the surrounding desert in every direction. The mountains had turned from pink to a soft lavender, and they appeared more reticulated and morphologically complex, deeper and more profound, than at midday. Between the two ranges the plain stretched hazy and indistinct, and he saw that it was scored by a lengthy purple infold whose depth the inspector was unable to tell. He turned the horse and was about to descend the rise on its gentler side when from the corner of his eye he caught sight of what he had been looking, though not hoping, to see. It might have been a dust devil, but the inspector, as he gazed, saw that, if so, it was a dust devil with a horse and rider like a tiny dark question mark at the center.

The inspector caught the horse behind the ribs with his heels hard enough to make it grunt as it skidded stiff-leggedly down through loose gravel to the hardpan desert floor. The spring had already recovered from their invasion, its riled waters clear and stilled. They thundered through it, raising silver splashes from the sand and flights of birds from the surrounding small trees, and deeper on into the fissure whose narrow walls seemed to close over their heads in a soft still twilight.

When they had gone a few hundred yards a faint trail appeared on the cañon floor, declining along the nearly imperceptible gradient. The inspector slowed the horse to a lope and held fast to the pommel as it sprang sideways to avoid small boulders and clumps of cactus and greasewood, its hooves setting up a deafening clatter within the narrow gorge. The wind that traveled lightly with them breathed in the oak trees sprouting from niches and benches cut into the rocky walls, and a pod of javelina broke in panic for cover ahead, brief gray forms smeared upon the green vegetation and the jumble of sand-colored rock.

Before they had gone very far the horse was winded and slackened its gait, and the inspector had to slash it across the rump with the ends of the reins to keep it at a brisk trot. The cañon continued to widen and deepen as they went, developing a crack in the clay floor that became a gulley descending by steps formed by accumulated piles of brush and stones to make a series of dry falls, and the more frequent trees stood taller beside boulders of increasing size. Each time the inspector attempted a backward glance over his shoulder he became dizzy and lost his balance in the saddle, until presently he no longer made the effort to look. The cañon was a crooked wedge of blue air beneath the yellow shine of the sky, and through this blueness the inspector made out ahead the restless green tumuli of big cottonwood trees turning over slowly on the down-cañon breeze.

Rufus backs stirred in the bushes beside the trail and along the cañon walls, and as they approached the trees a small herd of long-horn cattle appeared by a stock tank built of ax-hewn cottonwood planks caulked with pitch. The animals' spines showed like heavy chains coupling the hindquarters to the fore ones, their hipbones stuck out like tent poles, and the backs of several were freshly scarred by the claw marks of catamounts. The wetted cows backed and pawed and shook their horns threateningly at horse and rider as they went by. The horse sidestepped the cattle, but it did not bolt, and they trotted on, the inspector leaning forward above the neck to speak reassuringly to it. They passed under the heavy green foliage of the rough-barked cottonwoods where scarlet-and-black alder beetles swarmed and emerged from the trailing branches into sunlight again, with the cattle behind them and a circle of spring grass ahead. Crossing the grass the horse dropped its head, and the inspector, comprehending, gave it rein and allowed it to graze while he undid the saddlebag behind and drank some of the spring water which, though no longer cool, had retained its sweetness in the greasy bota. In spite of his fatigue his saddle-stiffness had left him as had his fear of the horse, with which he now felt almost entirely at ease. When he had drunk some water, though not as much as he had wished, he allowed it several minutes more to rest before kicking it into a reluctant walk.

The trail led across the grass into heavy brush that spread from one side of the cañon to the other, overgrowing boulders fallen from the rimrock above and talus slipped from the fracturing walls. The brush closed over the trail as high as the withers, but the horse pushed on through the seemingly impenetrable branches that parted about its shoulders, scraped the inspector's cotton legs, and closed behind them without a break, and almost without a tremor. They had nearly reached the apron of broken rock beneath the cañon wall when the inspector heard a crashing in the brush and, before he could look around, felt an impact that lifted the horse and him with it from the trail and impelled them forward in a breathtaking rush. The horse screamed once, gathered its feet under it, and made a leap that carried them squarely among the broken rocks, from which it sprang once more before going down. The inspector pitched headlong over its ears, turned three perfect somersaults in slow motion, and came to rest on an isolated patch of grass.

When he had regained his wind, he lay a little longer on his back staring up at the cliff top which appeared to be falling slowly backwards beneath an advancing scrim of evening cloud. Then he stood and turned to look for the horse. It was standing on three legs on the talus with its head dropped, breathing heavily and with a labored regularity. The inspector walked over and saw that the left foreleg hung from the shoulder, the hide pierced by splinters of raw bone and the torn tendons exposed amid oozing blood. He went round the horse and inspected the flank wound, which penetrated to the bone. The cow in withdrawing its horn had torn away a chunk of flesh and hide the size of a rump roast. The inspector took up the hanging reins and lifted the chin. The horse looked back at him from pain-dimmed eyes above which perceptible wrinkles had suddenly formed. He rubbed its nose with his knuckles and let the sad head droop again. The rigging was mysterious to him, but he set about unbuckling every strap he saw, and soon the heavy saddle came free in his arms and he let it flop down on the brittle rocks that in shifting made a sound like broken china under foot. From the saddlebags he extracted the bota and what remained of the tortillas in their waxed packets. He slung the bota by the cord about his neck and thrust the packets inside the cotton pants. The headstall came off easily over the ears, and the horse let the bit slip from its teeth as if it were life itself.

The inspector dropped the bridle on top of the saddle and hid everything in the brush. Then, without a backward look at the horse, he set off on foot down the cañon.

Limping and almost delirious from exhaustion, he emerged from the cañon into nightfall and found himself on the gravelly floodplain of a river that, flowing out from a cluster of volcanic cones, swung round before him in a hairpin curve and thence into the hills again in a sequence of braided rapids around sand and gravel bars. On the inside of the curve a cutbank stepped up to a sandy flat enclosed on three sides by the river and overgrown by a thick mesquite forest fifty or more acres in extent. The river eased into the hills and away again in a single gray unbroken piece except where the rapids riffled it, and the peaks of the hills glowed pink as they released their heat into the twilight sky from which the last cloud wisps had vanished. The inspector dropped down on the riverbank, peeled off what remained of the fouled socks, and thrust his torn, bleeding, stinking, bruised, pierced, and aching feet into the cool fast-moving water whose heavy burden of silt obscured them from his view. Keeping his feet in the water, he lay back on the sand with his arms against his sides and his eyes shut for some minutes. Then he sat again and massaged his feet for minutes more, splashing water high on his shins and soaking the legs of the cotton pants. Finally he arose, rolled the filthy socks into a ball, and walked upstream for several hundred feet until he came to a quiet and relatively shallow run that appealed to him as a likely crossing.

Once again water swirled and sucked around his legs, and the inspector winced with pain as his tortured feet bore upon the smoothly worn pebbles of the riverbed. He progressed by fits and starts, holding his elbows out and lifting his knees high, keeping his chin forward; his gestures stiff, exaggerated, and antic, like those of a mime. Three times he stumbled and nearly fell, cursing his agony, but each time he managed to recover his balance and went on. The water was colder than he had anticipated, producing a numbness that partially anaesthetized the pain. As he staggered from the river and onto the smooth and sandy bank, nighthawks flew and bats swooped in twittery patterns across the dusk. The inspector hesitated long enough for a backward look at the cañon, studying its shadowed mouth for the smallest movement. Then he went quickly on across the sand, climbed over the cutbank, and walked straight toward the gloom of the forest ahead.

The trees grew thickly above a deep carpet of dry leaves, but the inspector penetrated them as deeply as he could before the final light was absorbed into darkness beneath the canopy of branches. While his fear of snakes remained unabated and instinct warned him that he had arrived in a serpents' paradise, the need and desire for sleep overwhelmed him, removing every other consideration. He discovered by feel a thick trunk at hand and sat bracing his back against it. He drew the tortillas from his pants and ate the unstaled portion of the second one. When he had eaten he drank from the bota and hung it by its cord from a branch above his head. Lastly he pulled on the socks, stretched out in the leaves, and scuffed up a layer to cover himself from his chin down to his feet. The last things he knew were the whisper of the wind through the close small forest, the cries of nightbirds, and the distant run of the river like time behind the quiet night.

The inspector was awakened before sunrise by the cold and by hunger pains so acute that his first thought was that he was suffering an attack of appendicitis. Through the tops of the trees the sky looked an even gray as if it were preparing to rain, but when the sun rose not long after and seemingly all at once it revealed a domed sky like the inside of a steel bowl.

He stood stiffly, shedding leaves, and drank what remained of the water. Then he ate the molded remains of the tortillas very quickly and paying no attention to what he was eating. The leafy forest floor bore no trace of his passage across it, and he set off walking in the direction of the river sound that he was not aware of hearing until it occurred to him to listen for it. He reached the river in minutes but did not leave the shelter of the trees until he had carefully surveyed both banks and the cañon mouth beyond it. At last, moving carefully and using the forest edge for cover, he began to follow the river downstream, venturing onto the gravel plain only to fill the bota from a braid of the silty water.

When the mesquite forest petered out he kept to gullies and the dry beds of feeder creeks where he could, preferring these to the trackless gravel of the exposed riverbed. The sand was shallow, but as the sun got up it became a bed of wavery white light, scorching to his feet and blinding to his eyes. The inspector filled and refilled the bota from the river, and when he came to a bend where the brush overhung the current he climbed down into the water and immersed himself completely, letting the current sweep him along to the next overhang where he pulled himself up by handsful of thin branches and walked on, a figure the color of dirty salt, steaming as it strode beneath the corruscating desert sun.

All morning the inspector followed the river as it wound among the scorched hills where herds of free-ranging, half-feral cattle browsed the cactus scrub but saw no sign of human habitation, although once he came upon the oxidizing hulk of a motor vehicle set down and abandoned in the roadless wilderness as if by supernatural agency. By early afternoon he was unable to walk farther and dug himself a pit in the cool sand in the shade of an ironwood grove, where he slept for several hours until the declining sun struck at him at an angle between the branches and tortured him awake. The inspector refilled the bota from the river and started walking again.

Abruptly the river and he emerged together from the barren hills to face a man-made lake before them, its cobalt surface scarred by the chop of outboard motors. A mile farther on the river eased comfortably into the lake and the inspector set out around the western shoreline, which was crowded by unpainted shacks and piers collapsing into the water. People sat out in chairs on the piers eating their suppers, fishing, and listening to radio music turned loud. The inspector passed quickly behind the houses, keeping his head down, and was relieved when no one called out to him.

A fat young couple was having a fish fry in front of one of the last of the shacks. They moved inside as the inspector approached and he, altering course to cut across the dirt yard in front of the house, swiped a whole fish from the grill on the run. He heard the man shout and, for a time, the heavy tread and labored breathing of pursuit, before the sounds dropped farther and farther behind him and he concluded that he had safely outrun the fat man. The inspector jogged on for what he supposed to be a mile at least and presently entered a thicket of live oaks on the verge of a red clay bluff above the lake where, settling himself cross-legged among the leaves and sharp acorns, he devoured the fish. It was nearly a foot long from tail to gills: a carp, bug-eyed and rubber-mouthed, the pale flesh wormy and tasting of bottom mud and Crisco. He tossed the skeleton over his shoulder, and licked his fingers. The inspector looked longingly at the bed of leaves, but there was too much daylight left still and too many people about for him to lie down now. He rose from the leaves as if by a power extraneous to his will and shuffled on through the oak forest on aching legs, while gritting his teeth against the sharp rotating pains in his hip joints.

He walked right across the fire pit and over the pile of whited bones before he saw them. The pit was full of ashes, broken glass, and flattened tin cans, and the bones that were not scattered hung together in partial skeletons, some of them surmounted by branched antlers attached still to the bleaching skulls. The inspector regarded these things for a moment and was about to move on when he swung round and, returning to the camp, began to scavenge it fiercely on hands and knees. He worked rapidly and efficiently, running his hands under the leaves and sifting the ash and charcoal through his fingers with the aimless but intense optimism of a recreational shopper on Sunday afternoon, unaware of any particular need but confident that human ingenuity would furnish the object of his yet unidentified want. He found nothing however beneath the leaves or in the vicinity of the fire pit and, rising to his feet, was about to push on through the forest when he caught sight of a dark object juxtaposed with the white bones surmounting it. The inspector stepped forward and rolled the intact rib cage aside to retrieve the thing, which he recognized as the wooden handle of a knife from which the blade had been lost. He had not known that he wanted a knife, but the fact of finding a part—the useless part—of one in his hand made the lack seem suddenly a bitter one. In his disappointment he started to fling the handle among the branches of the live oaks, but dropped his arm in time. The evening sun through the trees gleamed along the parallel curves of the ivory cage at his feet, and the inspector, bend-ing, caught hold of the uppermost short rib and twisted it. The rib resisted before coming free in his hand with a cracking sound, and he studied it briefly end to end before carrying it to the fire pit, where he selected the flattest and smoothest of the fire-blackened rocks to work with.

It took him the better part of an hour to file the end of the rib to a lethal point and its base to the exact thickness required for a firm fit within the slot of the wooden handle, but when he was done the inspector had something resembling a paring knife, curve-bladed and evil-looking, that fitted easily beneath his cot-ton shirt or under the waist of the baggy pants. He inspected the job carefully. Then, after some hesitation and having drunk what water remained in the bota, he cut the leather bag into strips using a sharp piece of fire-hardened glass he found among the ashes and bound them tightly around the jointure of bone blade with wooden handle. The knife seemed to him sufficiently strong for a single well-placed thrust, and perhaps more than one.

A veil of indistinction had fallen between him and his handiwork, and the inspector, looking away from the knife, discovered that twilight had fallen through the roof of oak branches above his head and that he could no longer sit upright, pulled down by the welcoming earth beneath him. Well watered and with a bellyful of warm fish, no other need stood between him and the rest his tormented body craved and demanded. Stretched on his back, he drew up the leaves like a comforter and gazed at the emergent stars behind the dark pattern of oak cover. The stars grew rapidly larger and brighter, hurtling like intergalactic bullets toward a target appointed to them before time began, and the inspector, who had been half asleep, came to his senses with a start and seized the bone knife beside him. For several moments he lay rigid before his pounding heart subsided and his muscles relaxed. Then, carefully so as not to disturb the blanket of leaves, he tucked the knife into the top of his shirt and fell instantly asleep.

Thunderous reverberations awakened him to the expectation of rain, but a waning moon in a clear sky filled the oak forest with a silver light. The crash of a high-powered rifle was instantly followed by the same rolling echo as the inspector burst from his bed of leaves like a hairy hominid, clutching at his chest for the bone knife. When the rifle spoke again, he was already running bent over as if on all fours toward the edge of the bluff above the lake where a finger of light described a shallow arc along the shoreline. A hundred yards offshore a powerboat glided almost noiselessly at downthrottle behind a brilliant searchlight which, raising its trajectory, probed deep within the forest behind the bluff. The beam swung sharply round as the inspector flattened himself on the ground seconds before it cut like a machete through the branches directly above his head. Across the stillness of the water he could hear the sound of a rifle bolt being drawn back and the low voices of the poachers discussing where to throw the searchlight next.

Crablike the inspector scuttled backward on hands and knees into the forest where he regained his feet and moved cautiously toward the north end of the lake preceded by the powerboat moving in the same direction, careful to keep a hundred yards behind the searching wand of light. He and the boat had gone about a half-mile together when the searchlight cut suddenly back to the beach directly below him and held there. Immediately a large-bodied animal jumped from the spot and crashed upward in leaping bounds to the crest of the bluff and into the trees. The whine of the bullet came a second before the report from the water, and as the inspector stumbled and began to run fragments of branch and leaf torn by the second bullet struck him in the face, opening a small wound that sent a trickle of hot blood down his right temple. Believing that he had been mortally wounded the inspector halted in his tracks, expecting the imminent shutdown of his brain and the headlong fall of his carcass across the leaves. When to his astonishment neither event occurred, he ran on and broke from the forest into a small clearing where the searchlight caught and held him as if he had been a circus performer. His sudden appearance was greeted with angry shouts from the boat, followed by a volley of rifle shots that kicked up leaves and puffs of dust around him while the inspector did a brief but vigorous war dance, applauded by laughter and more shouts. The searchlight drifting behind a bosque beside the lake provided cover for escape as the inspector, regaining his composure, bounded away into the trees like a terrified deer.

At sunup he reached the cofferdam at the head of the lake and took up the track of the diminished river again as it renewed its course northward toward the international border.

The desert drew itself up from the valley into the foothills of the ranges east and west, and water flowed in the irrigation ditches on both sides of the river where the new crops filed away in fresh green rows between runnels of silver water. Privies at intervals lowered their backsides above the undercut banks a few yards distant from farmhouses surrounded by rusting farm machinery, derelict automobiles, and colorful laundry jigging on lengths of clothesline on a flat hard wind. The inspector increased his pace almost to a jog as he passed these houses, but the only human beings he saw were scantily dressed children who looked up briefly from their play to stare at him as he went by.

At midday he came to a dry wash in which he perceived fresh tire marks. He pursued these, and arrived shortly at a large trash dump bounded by a ring of oxidizing car bodies. The inspector rested briefly in the shade of a young cottonwood tree and then rummaged the dump, uncovering a pair of laceless boots with the heels gone and the half-soles worn through that he managed to patch with pieces of rotting wool from an old blanket. Also he found a book of paper matches only half used up. He would have searched further for other items of value, but the need for sleep overcame him. The inspector crawled inside the cab of a pickup truck faded to a sick tomato color and fell unconscious across corkscrew springs protruding from the ruined bench seat between the missing doors, through which only the slightest whisper of air passed. Not in his present lifetime, so it seemed to him, had he experienced the awful luxury of a real bed.

In his dreams he was being pursued across endless miles of scorching desert by a band of horseman visible on the horizon like a small black cloud, and when he awoke the wash lay in shadow and the sun was inserting itself into a notch in the western mountains. For a time he continued to lie on his back as he had awakened, staring at a malignant looking spider that peered at him from within a tear in the ancient felt lining of the steel roof, then eased himself feet foremost from the seat onto the firm sand of the arroyo that was still hot to his feet. The trash dump, a vast cornucopia, spread its wealth in piles around him. A noise as of a tin can dislodged sounded from one of the nearer piles, and then the inspector saw a long gray shape almost the size of a cat come scuttling along its edge.

He stopped working his toes in the sand and held his breath for as long as he was able before he heard more slippage from behind the pile, followed by the chink of a bottle dislodged. He slipped off the seat, picked up a short length of pipe lying at hand, and skimmed it across the top of the heap. More cans and bottles rained down, from which ten or a dozen rats fled scurrying up the wash and into holes dug high in its banks. The inspector found a chunk of concrete with a piece of rebar in it and flung that at the pile too; when no more rats ran out, he walked forward and began to dig again in the trash.

This time after seven or eight minutes of excavation he discovered a cookstove built of cast iron with a wide crack across the firewall and a half-length of broken stove pipe attached. He dragged the stove free of the pile, triggering a small avalanche behind it, and set it upright on its three remaining legs beside the pickup, taking care to position it so that he could stoke the fire and cook while sitting on the seat-end of the truck. Finally he climbed from the wash and went in search of firewood along the bank from which he returned dragging dead ironwood and mesquite branches, interrupting his work only to gather a handful of smooth round pebbles he placed in the torn pockets of the filthy cotton pants.

The inspector broke the branches he had brought and built a fire of them inside the stove, using pieces of cardboard, the rotten blanket, and handsful of dry grass for tinder. He worked as quietly as he could and when he had a strong fire going he sat in the pickup with a pebble in each hand and a small pile on the seat beside him and waited. Before he had waited very long, a rat showed its nose around the hulk of a coil refrigerator. The inspector stiffened, but forced himself to wait longer. As the rat crept forward, ears and whiskers twitching, he rose from the seat and in nearly the same single motion flung the stone he grasped in his right hand. After thirty-five years of disuse his pitching arm recalled its old training. The missile struck the rat behind the head and laid it out on the sand, the sleek pelt rippling over the erratically contracting muscles. The inspector replaced the second pebble in his pocket and retrieved the rat, lifting it gingerly by the tail. Since he had never before dressed game and had only the knife he had improvised for a tool, he made a messy and inexact job of the butchering. He placed the skinned corpse on the fire, roasted it for twenty minutes over coals, and ate with his fingers the tender meat that had something of the sweet rich flavor of pork. He ate about half the rat and placed the remainder in the cookstove with the still warm coals. While he was doing this, voices on the evening wind drifted down to him through the wash.

The inspector rose at once to his feet and stood listening. Then he began moving rapidly up the gulley, going bent over with his head below the level of the desert floor. The tire marks led on between the steadily lowering banks that forced him finally to a walking crouch and into a grove of cottonwoods veiled by the trailing green branches of the trees. The inspector went more slowly as he approached the grove and slipped carefully through the leafy screen, where old cans and broken bottles scuffed his new boots and plastic bags entrapped them. Now he could hear the voices quite plainly. Peering among the trees the inspector discerned the raw end of a potholed dirt street separating a row of wooden shacks from a vacant lot surrounded by a wire fence festooned with trash in which children played at stickball. Though the children were ragged and dirty their voices were strong, their bodies brown and well formed, robust. Three of them were boys, two girls. One of the girls, the prettier of them, pitched. She did not wind up to throw but swung her thin arm in a long arc behind her, brought it over her shoulder like a swimmer, and released the India rubber ball straight at the plate. The batter swung and missed while the other players watched him solemnly with their hands on their hips and their elbows out. The inspector from within the protective screen

87

of the trees watched them also, remembering the summer evening softball games of his youth in Spring Valley. The girl pitched the ball again, and again the boy swung and missed, too low this time and neglecting his follow-through. The inspector, almost bursting with enthusiasm, started to call out to the boy and restrained himself only in time. The first baseman ran to retrieve the ball and toss it back to the pitcher. The next time she threw less vigorously, and the mop handle connected with India rubber. Glancing from the wood, the ball arced gracefully backward over the batter's head as if aimed directly at the inspector's hiding place. He did not wait for them to follow but spun about and fought his way as fast as he could out of the cottonwood grove and into the ravine, through which he went limping in his new shoes on to camp.

The inspector waited nearly half an hour to kindle a second fire and sat watching from the truck seat as it blazed up within the cookstove, which cast an orange light behind itself through the wide open crack in the back. The dessicated branches burned rapidly, and he rose to throw on some more, enjoying the heat on his face as the air chilled rapidly with the advancing dusk. Iron mountains floated distantly on a ground haze that vanished at sunset, leaving the reticulated silhouettes sharp against a colored sky patterned with high cloud and smears of virga. Nameless flies fluttered across the shadows, and the eastern hills folded into themselves and flattened to a single dimension against a full moon rising. Sailing higher into the sky with an astonishing lightness, the moon transformed the inspector's dump into a glittering sculpture of mysterious complexity in which the cookstove appeared like a miniature temple enclosing its red votive flame. He was enjoying the spectacle of the fire as much as its warmth when the inspector gave a sudden snore and fell backwards upon the tattered upholstery, dead asleep.

He was wakened before dawn by the rats and climbed stiffly out of the wash in search of wood. In the thin gray light the inspector stumbled about, grasping at branches and fragments of decayed stump. Back at camp he took the matchbook from his pocket and found that two matches remained. He tugged a piece of cardboard box free of a Chevy engine block and pulled more handsful of the dry saltgrass, and when he reached to deposit the tinder within the cookstove a rattlesnake that had crawled inside for warmth during the night struck his forearm. The inspector flung the bitten arm up to protect his face and fell over backward onto the cold sand while the evil buzzing, amplified by the cast iron belly of the stove, persisted. He rolled several times more and, leaping to his feet, stared wildly around. Then he began running as fast as he could up the wash in the direction of the town, holding the arm high above his head like an Olympic torchrunner.

The distance was less than he remembered and he half expected to find the children still engaged in their game of stickball in the potholed street. Instead he discovered four Federales lounging and smoking cigarettes beside three army green lorries parked along the fence opposite the shacks. From narrowed eyes beneath the stiff visors of their military caps they observed the inspector as he ran toward them limping, his arms in the air. "There are men after me!" the inspector cried, addressing the one he recognized to be the captain.

The captain drew on his cigarette and stared as though he were inspecting a large and antic bug. "What did you do to make them wish to catch you?" he asked finally.

"Also I have been bitten by a rattlesnake!"

The captain dropped the butt into the road and turned the toe of his polished boot on it. "You have many troubles this morning, amigo," he agreed.

His sergeant took a new package from the pocket of his shirt, opened it, and offered the captain a cigarette. "There is a government clinic in town," he remarked.

"Will you drive me there please? Quickly! I am dying!"

The captain gave him a patient look, "Señor, we are here for a purpose. You think maybe we stand here for the good of our health, enjoying a cigarette, watching the trees grow?"

The inspector dropped his hand to his pocket. Then he took it away again. "I have been robbed, I tell you! I have no money!"

"The government clinic is in the Avenida Cinco de Mayo," the sergeant added.

The inspector looked from one to the other of the men. Then he turned and continued up the street, gripping his right forearm tightly with his left hand.

Smoke rose from the chimneys of the barrio and lowered again upon the roofs in an acrid pall. The inspector ran past a man asleep under a blanket on the ground surrounded by paper shopping bags, a toothbrush and razor, and a flock of chickens scratching and pecking the dirt, and came on a couple fornicating quietly in a sleeping bag. He passed them with his eyes averted, still at a run. Black-and-red Aztec buses stood on treadless tires before paintless motels surrounded by packed dirt, and beyond the motels immense flowerpots and other ceramic yard ornaments rested on fenced lots where old men boiled water in blackened kettles over burning sticks.

Traffic increased in the street, overlaying the smell of mesquite smoke with the strong fumes of leaded petrol. On the edge of the commercial district a vendor employed a short curved knife to pare the dripping red watermelon he pressed tightly under his arm. The inspector halted to ask the direction of the government clinic on Cinco de Mayo and, having received a blank stare in response to his question, trotted in desperation along the thoroughfare crowded with people and with trucks hauling baled hay and farm produce, Saltillo tile from Coahuila State, bricks, bottled gas, and coal. The small dark men and women he encountered, oblivious to his presence as to a ghost, failed to make way for him, causing the inspector on occasion to fall from the double stone step descending from the sidewalk to the gutter in his attempt to get round the unyielding pedestrians. Cast-iron lampposts bore overhead

wreathes from Christmases past. The inspector came to several
cross streets without finding Avenida Cinco de Mayo, but forbore
to inquire of two policemen in brown uniforms loitering with sinister negligence before the Banco Nacional de México with their
hands on their revolvers. Finally he approached a skinny old man
who stood against the window of a bodega plucking at the strings
of a tall golden harp. The man, without ceasing to play, gestured
with his head toward the next corner.

A crowd, many seated on campstools and folding chairs, waited
outside the clinic. The inspector made inquiries, and at last elic-
ited the information that the doctors never arrived before eleven
o'clock. "Pero dice el letrero, que a las ocho."

His informant gave him a close look. "Pues aquí así se hacen
las cosas." He shrugged.

"¡Pero . . . Pero . . . !" The inspector had no words to say that
a rattlesnake had bitten him. He stared around for help and saw
a woman with no legs sitting in a child's red wagon, a man with a
cancerous growth on one side of his face that had devoured an ear
and most of his nose. He saw people on crutches, people wrapped
in bandages caked with cheesy black blood, children with running
sores and noses that fouled their fronts with a livid snot. Before
him were ranged the sick poor of Mexico, dull-eyed and listless like
animals brought by their owners to be treated by the veterinarian.
The inspector sought the brightest pair of eyes, and in desperation thrust his wounded arm under them. The fang marks showed
livid against the pale skin, but he was astonished to see that major
discoloration and swelling had yet to occur. He guessed nearly an
hour had passed since he had been bitten. "Ah," the campesino
said. "Una serpiente. De cascabel. Fui mordido por muchas ser-
pientes. Déjame ver el brazo."

The old man put the pipe he had been holding between his
teeth and felt of the inspector's arm. His straw hat was discol-
ored and out at the crown, as if the coarse gray hair had punched
through it like spring grass. He placed a horny finger on the fang
marks and pressed delicately, pausing each time to observe the
patient's reaction. Finally he took the finger away, pushed the hat
back on his head, and looked the inspector in the eye. "No hay

91

hinchazón," he said. "Tiene mucha suerte."

"¿Qué dice?" the inspector felt cold all over and weak in the knees, comprehending that he stood now at the threshold of death. "¿Qué dice?"

Patiently the old man repeated his words until he made the inspector understand. He was lucky, a very lucky man, the campesino was telling him. Sometimes when the rattlesnake strikes it fails to inject venom, perhaps because it recognizes that the dose is insufficient to the size of the victim, perhaps because it strikes only in self-defense rather than from hunger. In any event, this particular snake had not poisoned him and so he was not going to die. He was not even going to be sick. Qué buena suerte.

The inspector rolled his sleeve down over the puncture wounds and withdrew his arm. He did not know whether he felt relief or anger, but he sensed the eyes of the old campesino on his back as he walked quickly away up the Avenida Cinco de Mayo.

The policemen in front of the Banco Nacional watched the inspector with hooded eyes as he approached the wide glass doors and passed through them into the bank. Across the parquet floor stained with tobacco juice, a pair of male tellers counted bills behind bulletproof windows, and plump women in parrot-colored dresses sat at plain steel desks beneath a mural depicting heroic peasants and workers being gunned down by robotic soldiers. The inspector stepped up to the woman at the head desk and explained to her that he was an American citizen from Nogales, Arizona, and wished to have money wired from his account there to the Banco Nacional. He spoke very slowly in halting Spanish while the woman listened, keeping her ear turned toward him and her eyes screwed. Her flowered dress exhaled a cheap perfume, and her bare forearms and upper lip were covered by a black down. When he had finished speaking, the woman unscrewed her eyes and straightened her head and told him that it was possible for her to do what he asked but that it would take a week to do it. The inspector explained that it was impossible for him to wait a week, that he needed the money no later than the following day, to which she responded with a shrug. "Lo siento mucho, señor. Éstamos en México." Replying to his inquiries, she added that he was one hundred kilometers from Nogales, that there was a daily bus to Benjamin Hill, and a train from there to the border. The inspector left the bank without thanking her and without acknowledging the two policemen, seated silently on the fender of a Porsche and tapping the ends of their truncheons against their polished black boots. Two blocks from the bank he was accosted by a ragged beggar and demanded of the man where he could obtain a free meal.

"Éstamos en México, señor. No hay tal cosa como la comida gratuita."

In despair, the inspector asked directions for the nearest church and started at once in search of it.

He crossed an imposing square bordered by whitewashed trees

93

and with a tall gazebo at the center of it and came to the church two blocks beyond the square. The small gray building bore no resemblance to the thick-walled, white-painted adobe churches of the tourist brochures; a renovative project had recently replaced the stonework on one side with sheets of pink marble, giving it the appearance of a partially skinned whale. Footworn steps rose to heavy wooden doors closed upon the twilit vestibule and past it the cavernous maw, ribbed with ancient timbers, of the church itself. The inspector went forward between the pews and the score of candles guttering in fruit glasses at the feet of Saint Mary and Saint Joseph to the sanctuary, where the holy flame burned evenly in a flume of red glass above the tabernacle. He tried the door to the sacristy and, finding it locked, walked back along the aisle to the vestibule where the plaster Christ swaddled in His burial clothes reposed in a catafalque of glass and wood surrounded by candles and vases of flowers real and artificial. The inspector put his shoulder against the half door, pushed through it—and spied parked across the street in the shade of a tree the red Chrysler sedan, wide and horribly faded and familiar beneath its torn Landau top.

The inspector ducked back into the church and hurried up the aisle again, holding his hand over his stomach as if he were going to be sick. He had just stepped up to the sanctuary when the door behind opened and a man stepped though it. "¿Qué quiere, señor?" the priest inquired.

Padre Tomás Velázquez, having put up the chalice and paten on the shelf and folded the corporal away after daily Mass, was letting himself out the back door of the church on his way to breakfast at the rectory when he heard someone try the door from the sacristy. He opened it and saw a man in filthy attire with a gaunt face and starving eyes looking at him. "¿Está necesitado?" Padre Tomás asked. Looking closer, "You are an American?" he added in surprise.

"Yes, American." The inspector, in spite of having eaten half a very large rat the evening before, felt suddenly faint with hunger. "Can I get something to eat here?"

"Of course. You may eat with me. I was just on my way to breakfast." The priest spoke perfect English without trace of accent. Standing aside, he invited the inspector to pass into the sacristy. "I am a poor cook," he apologized, "but even I can break an egg, and the ham is already cooked."

Hearing the words *egg* and *ham* the inspector nearly swooned, but he followed Father Velázquez along the concrete walk beneath the false orange trees, green bells of tight impenetrable foliage ringing with the song of innumerable birds, to the rectory. Once he looked back, and was relieved to see that he and the priest were hidden from the view of anyone who happened to be standing in the street. The rectory also was of gray stone, its narrow windows fitted with curving iron bars. The priest unlocked the door and stepped aside again to permit the inspector to enter.

The front room had white-painted walls and a tiled floor. It was furnished with a few chairs of tanned leather stretched over wooden frames, a low wooden table on which many books, magazines, and newspapers were piled, and a tall crucifix hanging forward from the wall at a rather threatening angle. In one corner of the room a green parrot about twenty inches long with a gray breast and an orange and red belly sat on a tall perch and cocked a round gray eye at the visitor. "You are not afraid of birds?" the priest asked. The inspector shook his head. At the age of eight or ten he had been taken by an aunt to a tea party where a huge crested parrot had swooped down on him while they were seated at table. In his terror he had dived beneath the table clutching the tablecloth, which brought down with it an avalanche of china, silver, and glassware, rich cakes and scalding tea. "A surprising number of people are," Father Velázquez remarked. "The Holy Ghost took a big chance when He came down on Our Lord in the form of a dove." He removed his cassock and hung it behind the door, and immediately the parrot flew from its perch onto his shoulder and commenced to groom the priest's heavy black beard. "We will eat in the kitchen if you don't mind," Father Velázquez said. "I'm sure you would like coffee. I have a few Kona beans left I brought with me from Hermosillo last month."

The inspector sat at table and leaned forward on the oilcloth. The puncture wounds in his arm ached, and his bones felt like water. He was expecting the priest to question him about himself, but Father Velázquez seemed entirely involved in the hand grinder and bringing water to boil in an ironware pot on the stove. While he worked the parrot flew off his shoulder to the countertop where it dragged paper toweling off the roller, tore away a piece and masticated it, and dropped the tiny wads like spitballs onto the floor. "When did you eat last?" Father Velázquez inquired.

"Yesterday evening. I had a rat for supper."

The priest added cold water to the pot and set it aside to let the grounds settle while he took the egg box from the small refrigerator. "Three eggs with your meat," he asked the inspector, "or more?"

"More please."

The priest lifted the iron skillet from its hook above the stove, rubbed it with butter, and laid in two slabs of rosy ham rounded by yellow fat. The parrot, watching him, commented frequently in a throaty, half-human voice, without words. Then he set the skillet on the flame and lifted the coffee pot. He added cream to the inspector's cup, and poured both cups full. "It's been quite a while since I ate an American breakfast," Father Velázquez said. "Ordinarily I have a roll and coffee in the morning. Have you lived a long time in Mexico?"

"About a week I guess. Maybe more."

"It is not easy for an American living in Mexico."

"Bandits took everything I had. My car. My money."

Father Velázquez sighed. "Mexico is getting better, but it will take time. It has been just ten years since we have been allowed to wear the collar in public. The new president is not a bad man. But Mexican law forbids him another term." He faced back to the stove again to turn the ham. "What did the police tell you?"

The inspector stared at the bottom of his coffee cup. "I haven't told the police. They're corrupt, aren't they?"

"It's really not all that bad." The priest brought the pot again. "I have only to scramble the eggs, and then we will eat. I think you ought to make a report to the police. I will drive you to the precinct house after breakfast, if you wish."

Father Velázquez filled the plates and spoke a word in Spanish to the parrot, which flew onto the back of one of the table chairs. Then he carried the food to the table and sat opposite the inspector, who began to eat even before the priest had finished saying grace. "Bless us O Lord and these Thy gifts which we are about to receive from Thy bounty, through Christ our Lord, amen." The golden eggs nearly covered the meat on his plate, a country ham from which a few stiff bristles yet protruded. When the priest cut his first piece of meat, the parrot flew down to the table and, having seized it in its beak, pulled it from the plate and devoured it, holding the morsel clenched in one pink claw as Moses once had grasped the Tablets.

The inspector ate ravenously and drank off the pot of coffee. When he had finished eating he was so sleepy that he could barely remain upright in the chair. "The bed is made up in the guest room," the priest said. "I will be away all morning, but after lunch I will drive you to the precinct station—if you wish to make a report, of course. My secretary's name is Linda Chávez and the caretaker is Manuel, her husband. I will ask them to be careful not to disturb you. When you bathe, please remember that we are extremely short of water here."

In the cabinet-sized bath the inspector stripped off the little that remained of his clothes and rubbed himself down with a small cake of homemade soap under a shower of tepid water that circled in black counterclockwise whorls around his feet above the slow drain. He dried off with a thin towel skimpily napped and applied alcohol from the medicine cabinet to the angry-looking punctures in his forearm. Then he returned to the bedroom and threw himself on the bed across the turned-down sheet without bothering to get under it. He slept, and dreamed he was lying on the seat of the stripped pickup truck surrounded by mountains of trash as the moon rose, sealing the rough surface of the desert with the strong protective beauty of its unearthly light.

When the inspector awoke he knew by the tired quality of the light that it was evening and that he had slept through the entire day. His hair was matted where it had dried on the pillow, and his naked body above the sheets felt slightly chill. A Bible rested on a table by the bed, and when the inspector rolled over his gaze met a stark black crucifix on the wall above the headboard. Feeling weak but reconstituted, he went into the bathroom where he took a drink from the tap and applied more alcohol to the snakebite. When he came out of the bath clean trousers, a shirt, and socks had been placed on a chair against the wall, with a pair of oxfords in approximately his size resting beside the chair. The inspector sat a long time on the edge of the bed before he started to dress, and by the time he was finished the light was so dim he had to switch on the bedside lamp. Thoughtlessly he took up the Bible, opened it at random, and read, translating slowly, "Blessed are you, Father, Lord of heaven and earth; for although you have hidden these things from the wise and learned, you have revealed to little ones the mysteries of your kingdom." He turned off the lamp, left the bedroom, and followed the hall out to the sitting room, where Father Velázquez was seated in twilight in an armchair reading the evening Office. The priest set the breviary aside as the inspector entered the room. "Good evening," he said. "I hope you slept well today?"

"I'd say I did. I bet I never turned over once."

"I considered waking you when I came in, but Linda said she hadn't heard you up a single time, and I thought it better to let you sleep."

"I'm glad you did."

The priest pulled the cord on the standing lamp beside him and studied the inspector, carefully but with tact, in the ruddy light passed by the leather shade. "You *look* much better, anyway," Father Velázquez said. "Do you feel up to a cocktail tonight?"

"*My God yes!*"

The sitting room was comfortably furnished with potted plants in the corners, Zapotec rugs on the walls, and a few pieces of Aztec sculpture placed here and there. The parrot, which had been asleep on the corner of the mantelpiece, took its head from under its wing and fixed the padre with a jealous eye. "Do you prefer gin or tequila?" Father Velázquez asked. "My American friends always drank bourbon, but as long as I was in the States I was never able to acquire a taste for it."

"You lived in America, then?"

"I was trained at a seminary near Hartford, Connecticut. You're not a Catholic? You would be surprised to learn how many candidates from Latin and South America are being trained for the priesthood in American seminaries, partly because so few American young men nowadays are interested in a vocation. How does gin and tonic sound?"

"Wonderful, thank you."

Father Velázquez brought tall glasses with ice from the kitchen and a whole lime. He poured gin from a lead-crystal decanter standing on a silver tray on the sideboard into two glasses and added tonic water and cut two thick wedges from the fruit, leaving the rest for the parrot to wrestle with and finally destroy while the two men settled themselves with their drinks in facing wicker chairs. "Were you on your way home when the bandits robbed you?" Father Velázquez inquired.

"Yes."

"And where *is* home? If I may ask."

"Nogales."

"Arizona."

"Yes."

"I will give you the money you need to get home on."

"I'll send a money order as soon as I get there."

"If you like. I do have an indigent fund available."

"You must be the most popular man in town."

"The Church is popular in Mexico even when She is poor. Except among the politicians."

The inspector's mind wandered. Once again he was on the red mesa above the camp with Jesús and María and the expatriate, hearing the wind thresh the forest of dark little trees. It was the

100

gin, he realized after a moment, which had the same pungent savor as juniper. "Linda left us a cold chicken for supper," the priest was saying. "I presume you're planning on staying the night. In the morning I will drive you to the bus. There are two trains a day from Benjamin Hill to Nogales."

"That's very good of you. Do you make a habit of putting up total strangers in your house?"

"At night I sleep with the bedroom door locked. It is not only lost American tourists that bandits rob and kill. I warned Manuel this morning you might be a prisoner escaped from the federal prison at Hermosillo. Manuel is a former prizefighter and very fast with a revolver."

"Do you believe that I am an escaped prisoner?"

"No. I believe you are running either from or toward something—maybe both. What, I do not care to guess."

"All I want is to get home safely."

"That is what I want, too. May I freshen your drink before we eat? Sansón has stolen the rest of the lime. I will bring another."

They ate at a mahogany table that occupied most of the plainly formal dining room, facing one another across a pair of silver candlesticks and a large silver bowl. Father Velázquez was in his late thirties with a smooth complexion, dark skin, and no gray as yet in his black hair and beard. For supper they had an Indian soup made with sliced avocado and tomatoes, corn tortillas, cold roast chicken, and cold pinto beans. The wine, poured by the priest into fluted glasses, was an excellent dry Chilean white. The inspector thought this by far the most elegant meal he had ever eaten, but he could not help being scandalized by such luxury enjoyed by the clergy in the midst of almost universal want and dire poverty. Candlelight circumscribed the silver bowl along its edge, wavered on the polished wood, and illuminated a ceramic tree set on the sideboard. The tree, three or three-and-a-half feet tall, swelled from a bell-shaped base in a spreading pattern of trunk, branch, and leaf entwining a variety of figures that included Adam and Eve and the Serpent, strange and surprising flowers, butterflies, fantastical birds, and Christian saints. The inspector was several times on the point of asking the priest what the tree was meant to represent, but being unable sincerely to admire the hideous thing, he held his tongue. At the end of the meal Father Velázquez tossed a leg bone onto the floor for the parrot, which landed on it with a loud screech and proceeded to ride the bone across the floor as if it were a scooter.

Together they cleared away the plates and carried them to the kitchen, and the priest asked the inspector if he cared to accompany him to the church to prepare for morning Mass. The inspector, from politeness, said he would be happy to do so, and the two set off along the winding path under the silent orange trees in the darkness. The street was empty save for a young couple progressing slowly, as a single form, from one circle of lamplight to the next, and now and then a car passed by, its radio blaring corrido. When they reached the back door of the church the priest drew an immense latchkey from under his cassock and inserted it in the lock, which clanked and groaned anciently as if it guarded the Roman Catacombs.

In the sacristy Father Velázquez took the chalice and paten from the cupboard, filled a glass dish with water, and laid out a fresh corporal and napkin. He brought out the jug of red wine and the jar containing the unconsecrated hosts. While he was doing these things the inspector wandered into the church where, standing alone by the pulpit looking up the shadowy nave, he found himself thinking of María for whom he had promised to pray. After some hesitation he began a reluctant prayer and was immediately overwhelmed by mortification, like a man caught performing an act completely out of character in full public view. The inspector was about to turn back to the sacristy when a low moan sounded from the darkness and he noticed for the first time a figure kneeling at the side of the church before the fluttering candles. As he watched the woman cried out again and prostrated her enormous bulk upon the stone floor.

The priest glided silently from behind him, descended the steps, and went straight toward the woman. Reaching her he extended his hand and helped her to rise first to her knees and next, after a struggle, to her feet where she stood swaying, an obese woman in the final stages of pregnancy. The woman listened

102

quietly as Father Velázquez spoke to her, and then she began to cry again. Father Velázquez put his arm about her shoulders as, speaking in a voice that remained inaudible to the inspector, he led her up the aisle to the front of the church. When they came to the big wooden doors the priest opened one of them and ushered the woman gently out into the night. He locked the doors and returned to the sacristy where the inspector awaited him. "What was the matter with her?" the inspector asked.

"Ana lost a child last year. It was her twentieth. As you could see, she is pregnant with her twenty-first."

"Twenty children? A poor woman like that? What does her husband do for a living?"

"Her husband was invalided ten years ago in a mining accident. She is from a large family herself."

"But *why*?"

Father Velázquez had the big key in his hand again. The inspector saw that it was attached to a ring from which two other keys of equal size hung. "Children are a blessing from God," he said. "But the Church teaches that restraint is as necessary as procreation. The difference between your country and mine is the difference between abstraction and nature, brains and genitalia. When these things are brought together again instead of being kept apart, then Mexico and America will no longer be so far from God, and perhaps much closer to one another, as well."

Again from politeness the inspector attended Father Velázquez's Mass at seven in the morning together with a few old women, some grizzled campesinos, and in their midst the wife of one of the local ricos: a beautiful lady in her late twenties wearing a lavender silk dress, lavender shoes, and heavy gold bracelets, accompanied by two perfect children below the age of ten. After Mass he and the priest ate a breakfast of freshly baked rolls, oranges, and black coffee, and then the inspector went to the guest room for the kit bag Father Velázquez had given him containing toiletries and some money. Having washed his hands and applied cologne lightly to his chin and neck, the inspector lifted the mattress, drew from beneath it the knife he had fashioned from the deer's rib, and placed it in the satchel with the other things. Then he left the rectory and walked around to the driveway, where Father Velázquez sat in his white Ford sedan with the engine running.

The Aztec bus waited, surrounded by people eating tamales and apple pastries while they prepared to board. The pneumatic door was sealed and the operator nowhere in sight. "I would be happy to wait with you," the priest said, "but I must take Communion to the hospital patients. Are you certain that you have enough money?"

"I have plenty, Father. I'll repay you by wire within forty-eight hours."

"There is no hurry. If you find it more convenient, donate the amount to a parish on the American side."

"But what you have lent me is Mexican money."

"The Church is not divided by international boundaries, Mr. White."

"But American money will go so much further in Mexico."

Father Velázquez gazed across the street to a stonecutter's shop where artisans like pale grotesque angels worked in a pall of rock dust, carving tombstones from large blocks of granite. "Even in Mexico, money simply gets in the way at times. American money especially." The priest checked his watch. "The bus is always an hour late at least in leaving, often two hours. There is a coffee shop around the corner. Vaya con Dios."

"Vaya con Dios, Padre."

He did not go to the coffee shop for fear that the driver would return suddenly and drive away without him. The inspector stood with the other passengers on the glaring sidewalk, and presently a campesino approached to offer him a warm coca from the net shopping bag he carried on his arm. The inspector was about to refuse him when, to his own surprise, he accepted the can instead and drank from it while the campesino and everyone else watched with grave expressions. More passengers arrived, accompanied by vendors hawking pastries, candy, and hot coffee. At last a short, heavyset, and scowling man wearing a too-tight uniform unlocked the door and climbed up into the driver's seat where he shut the door again by automatic control and sat for a time as if asleep. At last he reopened the door, climbed down from the bus, and began placing luggage in the hold as he took money and gave out tickets. The driver stowed the caged chickens below and passed the trussed ones into the coach with their owners, along with a couple of goats and a shoat that squealed like a fire siren. The inspector, having no luggage to check, was the first person permitted to board. He chose the bench seat directly behind the door and sat pressed against the window while the other passengers, human and animal, struggled past him, sweating in the close heat of the bus. His seat mate, an old man smelling of onions and chewing tobacco and with an ugly growth on the inside of his hanging lower lip, shook out a crumpled newspaper and applied himself to the sports pages.

Across the aisle a young woman held the terrified shoat to her breast as tenderly as if it were a child. Most of the windows in the bus were jammed shut, and just when it seemed to the inspector that the heat and the closeness and the pandemonium had become unbearable the driver climbed to his seat and shut the pneumatic door. The bus lurched forward and drew away from the curb. It was attempting to force its way into the traffic when a man appeared dodging among the cars and trucks, shouting and waving at the driver who paid him no attention. The man was tall and well built, with long hair falling from under his battered dusty sombrero and long whiskers. As he passed in front of the windshield he pounded on the glass with his fist until the driver, cursing, threw the lever that operated the door. The tall man entered the bus in a single leap that put him directly beside the driver, who accepted his money silently and received no word in return. He turned and sat down on the step facing the door with his feet in the stairwell directly beneath the NO FUMAR sign and the inspector's horrified stare. The driver, paying no attention to the sign, drew a cigarette from his pocket and lit it.

The bus pulled forward among the lesser vehicles, the driver leaning on the horn for emphasis and employing brake and accelerator recklessly so that men, women, and animals cried out together as they were flung violently forward and backward in the hard seats. Once past the outskirts of the town it went faster and faster in the narrow highway, hurtling into the unbanked curves without slackening speed and passing cars and large trucks across a solid yellow line. The countryside became a blur in which objects were distinguishable for seconds only, like flotsam borne on the crest of a raging flood. By leaning outward from his seat the inspector was able to read the speedometer, which registered above 150 kilometers an hour. In his fright he nearly forgot the expatriate, who continued to sit very still with his head down and without ever looking up from the well. By the time the bus made its first stop the inspector was weak and shaking and his new clothes were drenched with perspiration. People crowded forward, and the expatriate, his face hidden by the hat, stepped down and stood against the side of the bus to smoke a cigarette as the passengers disembarked on the village square and were met by relatives waiting with jalopies and pickup trucks assembled from parts taken from trucks of a similar model and held together by spot welds, steel wire, and bailing string. As soon as they were off the bus the expatriate stepped up again, passed by the inspector without looking at him, and pushed his way on to the rear, followed by the boarding passengers. Then the driver got behind the wheel again and the bus rattled forward across the cobblestone square.

Traffic over the next stretch of road was considerably heavier, but the driver seemed oblivious, twice pulling into the oncoming lane to pass on a steep hill. Just past the summit of an arched bridge over an arroyo they met a lorry head-on while getting round a crowded school bus. The driver put the brake pedal to the floor and nearly sideswiped the bus while attempting to drop back into his lane as the school-bus operator, hoping to disengage his vehicle from the impending catastrophe, accelerated on the downslope past the lorry, leaving a vacuum into which the Aztec was able to slip barely in time to avoid collision. The inspector laid his head against the window and closed his eyes as the old man beside him crossed himself and cut a fresh chew. As they entered the next village the driver swerved deliberately to nudge with his fender a cyclist peddling along the edge of the road, sending him and his machine airborne through the sunshine, end over end against the white sky before the two separated with technical precision and crashed at last upon a thin mattress of creosote bush.

They reached Benjamin Hill shortly after noon and almost two hours behind schedule. Since, however, the afternoon train to Nogales did not depart until three o'clock the inspector's connection was not jeopardized. The bus stop was downtown but otherwise appeared to have been chosen for no particular reason of convenience. The inspector kept his seat while the passengers departed with their livestock, and only when he calculated that everyone must have disembarked did he lift his head and look cautiously around. The aisle was littered with candy wrappers and goat dung; except for a pair of trussed chickens left behind on the overhead rack, he was alone on the bus. Through the filthy window he surveyed the milling crowd, and discovered the expatriate missing from it.

The inspector kept his seat until the people had dispersed with their baggage and the driver climbed up to retrieve the chickens, scowling at finding him still on board. He ignored the man and, stepping down to the sidewalk, looked carefully along the street where a few desultory pedestrians ambled and an automobile burned quietly by itself against the curb a block and a half away. The inspector put his head inside the bus again to ask directions to the train station, but the driver pretended not to understand him, and so he set off up the street toward what he took to be the business district. He had gone only two blocks when the driver of a passing taxi hailed him.

"¿Adónde vas, amigo?"

"A la estacíon."

"Bueno, vamos."

"¿Cuanto cuesta?"

"Para tí, amigo, seis dólares."

"No tengo dolares."

"Pues diez pesos."

The driver made a U-turn in the street with his fare, drove two blocks past the Aztec bus, turned the corner, went another block, and pulled up in front of the railway station.

The inspector paid the fare and entered the station which was empty except for a small thin man making sad circles with a broom over the gray stone floor. The window was drawn down below the BOLETOS sign. He crossed the waiting room and stepped onto the platform where a dozen Central American refugees sat on folding chairs surrounded by tied bundles and staring across the tracks like starved Buddhas. Twists of human excrement baked on the concrete surface and gathered flies. The inspector went into the station again to use the restroom but found it locked against an overpowering reek of stale urine. A nearly illegible notice handwritten on a chalkboard appeared to announce that the train would be late; he could not tell by how much. He seated himself on a circular bench at the center of the waiting room and counted his remaining money. The paper bills illustrated in sepia shades and the thick fingersome coins seemed excruciatingly foreign; Nogales, Arizona, infinitely far away. The inspector put the money back into the kit bag and concentrated on watching the small brown birds flying into the station through the grimy louvered windows, and out of it again.

A band of Tarahumara Indians was gathered to meet the southbound train. The women wore traditional dress except for the American jogging shoes, but the children went barefoot, their soles glimmering palely behind them as they walked. Several of the men carried boom boxes, and each had over his arm the frayed gray jacket emblematic of Mexico's male poor. The adults squatted together along the wall of the station, while two small girls played a game with an empty tequila bottle and a small boy wearing a pair of eyeglasses on a black cord strutted up and down the waiting room crying, "Extra! Extra!" pretending he had newspapers to sell. As the inspector watched, a small European car polished to a high gloss stopped in front of the station, and a lady climbed out from it.

She was a fine-looking Spanish woman, elegantly dressed and with the assurance of a person well accustomed to summoning order out of chaos. Her gaze cut across the waiting room—the Tarahumara, the inspector, the closed ticket window—and lingered upon the slate board with its chalked semiliterate scrawl. Almost without breaking stride she marched across the station, rapped smartly on a small unlettered door, and collared the uniformed official who emerged from it and with whom she conversed for some seconds before crossing directly over to the inspector, still watching from his bench. "The train is delayed until four-thirty," the lady said crisply. "The ticket window will not open until four. Give me the money, and I will buy your ticket now from the stationmaster. There are only thirteen seats remaining on the train."

She was gone several minutes and returned with the tickets in her hand. "Probably the train was stopped north of Guadalajara by bandits, or by the police checking the baggage car for drugs someone did not want to pay off on. Do you see those Guatemalans on the platform? They are on their way through Mexico from the southern border to enter your country illegally. It is still two hours before the train arrives. We have time for lunch if you are hungry. There is one good restaurant in town, and my nephew will be happy to drop us there." Through the plate-glass window the inspector saw the expatriate pass by on the platform and seat himself with the Guatemalans. "I'm hungry," he said.

The lady introduced herself as Cruz Beatriz Kattán-Ibarra, and her nephew as Hernando Cristóbal Ordóñez. The inspector tried to concentrate on the conversation during the brief ride to the restaurant but thoughts of the expatriate distracted him. The nephew was a slim, tall, good-looking young man wearing an American sports shirt, pressed chino slacks, and tortoise-shell glasses, soft-spoken and very polite, who greatly admired America where he had attended parochial school in Nogales and hoped to earn a degree in business administration at Harvard University. America was the future of the world, he believed, and the coming generation in Mexico was preparing to lift their country out of Third World poverty and ignorance by copying American business methods and the American political system and ridding itself of feudalism and superstition. "Mexico," he said, "needs to get real. Don't you agree, sir?" The inspector, who had turned to look back through the rear window, said that indeed he did agree. To his enormous relief, no one was following behind the car.

The restaurant was a one-story adobe building painted pale blue, with shuttered windows and a recessed doorway in which a crudely stenciled menu was displayed in a glass case. Beatriz Kattán-Ibarra and the inspector got out at the curb, and the nephew promised to return for them at a quarter past four. The house, built as the private residence of a wealthy copper miner in the 1860's, though renovated remained fundamentally intact, retaining the original walls, hardwood floors, and vigas. A massive armoire dominated a wide hallway separating adjacent dining rooms opening off on either side. Señora Kattán-Ibarra's heels struck sharply upon the polished wood between the throw rugs, and instantly a small man wearing a rusty dinner jacket appeared behind a lectern on which the reservations book, illuminated by a small brass lamp, was spread. "Oh, Señora," he exclaimed, "perdóneme la espera."

"No importa, Alfredo. Tenemos mucho tiempo."

Alfredo led them past the bar where the barman sat reading a newspaper to one of two back rooms where he drew out two chairs from the best table and stood behind the señora's while she seated herself. "Dos vinos blancos, por favor," she told him. The restaurant had no other guests than themselves. "Alfredo's was always the fashionable place for lunch," Señora Kattán-Ibarra explained, "until the big American motel opened here two years ago. Now the wealthy businessmen in Benjamin Hill take their clients there."

Alfredo came with the wine and offered to take their order, but Beatriz Kattán-Ibarra said that they were in no hurry and preferred to delay. He bowed and disappeared; almost at once a piano struck up from one of the front rooms. "They still have music here in the evenings," the señora remarked. "Alfredo is an aficionado. His mother was born in Italy."

"Do you live in Benjamin Hill?"

"No. I live in Nogales, Sonora, where I bought a house ten years ago when my children began to attend St. Mary's Catholic school on the American side. In those days parochial schools were outlawed by the Mexican government. Now that Napoléon and Conchita are grown, I plan on selling the house and moving back to Hermosillo to be near my late husband's family. Nogales has become very filthy and crowded with Guatemalans and Indians trying to enter the United States. The sewage system is dangerously overstrained; health officials are warning of the possibility of a cholera epidemic soon."

"I lived on the Arizona side for twenty-five years."

"You know, then." The pianist began a Chopin waltz, and Señora Kattán-Ibarra made a face. "They used to find better talent than that," she said. The inspector, never having heard of Chopin, did not offer an opinion. "At the motel they have a rock band every night. Mexico has become dreadfully Americanized in the last twenty years."

The inspector was offended. "Is that such a bad thing, do you think?"

"In many ways, yes. Mexico is *meant* to be Mexico, not a third-rate copy or approximation of some other country."

"Your nephew would disagree with you."

"Hernando is young and has a great deal to learn yet about his country. And yours."

111

The pianist started another waltz, causing Señora Kattán-Ibarra to grimace again. The inspector listened, trying to discover in the music the cause of her distress. Alfredo brought two glasses more of the dry white wine and stood behind the lady's shoulder with his pad and pencil ready while they ordered from the carte du jour. "Ponga a prueba a la pianista con otra pieza," the señora told him. "Algo mas facilito."

Alfredo shrugged. "¿Facilito como qué? Ella es no muy consumada."

"¿Pues por ejemplo, conocerá ella acaso a Carlos Gardel?"

"Se lo pregunto."

He vanished, and presently a tango commenced in the front room. Beatriz listened with her head bent to one side, holding the slim stem of the wineglass between her crimson nails. "Better," she admitted. "But he is merely being polite by auditioning her further."

When Alfredo brought the meal the inspector regarded his plate apprehensively. He had ordered cabrillo because he was equally unfamiliar with the other dishes on the menu and because Beatriz had ordered it for herself. It was a grilled fish of some kind he saw, served with a butter-and-lemon sauce, asparagus, and boiled new potatoes: all a considerable surprise to the inspector, for whom Mexican food meant tacos and refried beans. "Alfredo has the fish flown in daily from Guaymas," Beatriz told him. "His produce he buys from my in-laws' farms near Hermosillo. My husband first brought me to dinner here twenty-one years ago when he became the restaurant's supplier. Benjamin Hill is not a town anyone is likely just to jump off the train and visit."

The wine he had consumed gave the inspector the courage to ask the question he had been considering since he watched Señora Kattán-Ibarra stalk across the station and collar the railroad official. "How can a person like you," he inquired, "stand to live in a place like Mexico?"

Her eyes above her lifted fork clearly expressed her wish to put him on the spot. "What kind of person is a person like me? And what kind of a place is Mexico?"

The inspector fumbled his own fork and dropped his eyes in abashment. "Well you, you know, you're very . . . civilized. And

112

Mexico is so *un*-civilized."

Beatriz Kattán-Ibarra set her fork down beside her plate. "Do you know why I offered to buy your tickets at the station? It was because even more so than most Americans, you looked so innocent—helpless, almost. Of course I know you're *not* helpless—that was only an impression of mine, not an objective perception. So you find Mexico uncivilized?"

Alfredo brought two more glasses of wine, and the inspector pounced gratefully upon his. "Well, I mean . . . relatively speaking, you know."

"Relative to the United States, do you mean? You needn't be embarrassed, I'm not offended in the least. I'm not an apologist for Mexico; I don't care what the yanquis—or anyone else— think of my country, but I do resent their not making the effort to see it for what it actually is. And what it is, is neither a Third World society trying to 'develop' in imitation of what is called the 'American model' nor a socialist machine for the production of a mass proletariat eager to swarm over the United States like a plague of locusts, though this proletariat does in fact exist today. What will happen to it I don't know, and anyway it doesn't matter much. Probably they will all starve to death eventually, either here or in the U.S. They are the direct result of the revolution, and the revolution now is over, is dead. But you Americans—you see this ragged mob jostling and pushing across the border, and you think well, here's Mexico, coming our way. But they are *not* Mexico—not the true and indestructible Mexico. Only a rather dreary moment in Mexico's long, bloody, and very beautiful history.

"Mexico is a civilization and has been one for five hundred years. America by comparison is merely modernity, a stage in history constructed from a theory that enough people have believed in long enough and hard enough to give it a transient appearance of reality that has already begun to fade. America is a sentimentality, based on related sentimentalities like technological efficiency and the betterment of man. Whereas Mexico is an expression of human truth: a thin crust of culture and wealth above a morass of ignorance and barbarism, courage and endurance, where people are not afraid to confront the reality of life and death. Long after

113

the United States and its antiseptic culture have ceased to exist, the *real* America will survive—here, and in the South, and maybe even in the reconquered territories in the North. Do you think the reconquista is a dream? I myself believe that Mexico is only dreaming the conquista, and that, once we all awake, it will be to the eighteenth century or the seventeenth, not the twentieth."

They finished lunch to the background accompaniment of clumsily executed tangos. Beatriz after checking her watch said they had time for a last glass of wine; already the inspector's cheeks were flushed and his mind enflamed. Alfredo brought coffee and retired to write up the bill. While he was away women's shoes tripped in the hall, and a lovely girl entered the dining room. She stood poised beyond the threshold, lifting her chin and working her long white fingers athletically as she gazed about for the patrón. Then with utter composure she walked rapidly over to the inspector and, without acknowledging the presence of Beatriz Kattán-Ibarra, asked him in a clear low voice, "You liked my playing—yes?"

The inspector stared at her, at loss for an answer.

"Thank you," the girl said, and gave him a smile like a sunrise. "You will tell the patrón how you enjoyed me, no?" She raised her beautiful head to catch the incoming light from the windows that glowed in the ends of her Spanish gold hair. "He is coming now," she said in a whisper. "It will mean so much to him, and to me—yes?"

Alfredo came forward with the bill face down on a silver plate and set it before him on the linen cloth. The inspector turned the paper over and saw to his horror that it was for several times the sum of money in his pocket. In his humiliation he pushed himself away from the table and, raising his hands to the girl, began to applaud loudly. "¡Bella música! ¡Bella música!" the inspector cried loudly—too loudly, he realized. "¡Bella música! ¡Bella, bella, bella!"

The radiant look he received from the girl, though gratifying, was small compensation for the disdain he read in Beatriz Kattán-Ibarra's aristocratic face as, with two slender fingers, she lifted the bill from the plate and paid the full amount in the crisp sepia currency of the Republic of Mexico.

114

At the station they found the train already waiting and, having made up a full thirty minutes in schedule, preparing to depart fifteen minutes in advance of the revised one. Beatriz and the inspector flung themselves from the car shouting goodbyes to the nephew and tore across the waiting room and onto the platform, where the inspector turned his ankle in a pile of human dung as they dashed toward the nearest coach. The train was in motion as they climbed the steps to the vestibule, which was crowded by people unable to find seats inside the coach. "Have you traveled before in Mexico by second-class train?" Beatriz asked. "The travel agencies, and even the Ferrocarriles Nacionales, pretend it doesn't exist so far as foreign tourists are concerned. But, as you are about to discover, it is one of the glories of our federal republic. If I were not in a hurry to get home this evening, we would have waited for the first-class train from Guadalajara in the morning." The inspector, scraping shit from the side of his shoe while he stared above the crowd for sight of the expatriate, did not reply to her.

"Follow me!" Beatriz spoke sharply, and he kept obediently behind her as she forced her way among her placid and sweating compatriots into the coach where passengers sat on their luggage in the aisle drinking cocas and eating tacos and manalones purchased from vendors with their wheeled carts and bicycles parked between the train and the southbound track. The first seats on both sides of the car beyond the vestibule had been claimed by the conductor, his wife and three daughters, and a large green trunk from which he dispensed coffee poured from thermoses into styrofoam cups. The luggage racks were crowded with shapeless bundles tied with string and cardboard boxes packed with pails of lard and ham sandwiches wrapped in clear plastic. Beatriz secured the armrests at the ends of the two rows of seats beyond the conductor's family and stowed her overnight bag on the floor between her ankles. A woman in the next seat up cradled a kitten in her arms. She smiled at the inspector suddenly, and he from self-consciousness looked away to find all three of the conductor's daughters staring at him in fascination. Caught out, the girls turned their heads quickly and hid their faces on each other's shoulders. The inspector drew a few coins from his pocket and bought coffee for himself and Beatriz. The black coffee, though strong, was nearly half sugar. When he attempted to return the cup for a refill the conductor at first gestured impatiently, then seized it and flung the cup through the open window before filling a new one. Beatriz refused more coffee. She sat quite still with her pocketbook in her lap and her hands folded upon it as she stared at the passing countryside streaked by lengthening shadows, seemingly oblivious to the pressing humanity about her.

The train rocked leisurely northward in a cloud of diesel smoke and the reek of overheated brakes. At every hamlet it stopped and was boarded by women who came pushing though the coaches offering tamales and apple pastries from tin buckets while their men paced the train in pickup trucks along the access road running parallel to the tracks. At the next village the women disembarked, and another group of vendors climbed aboard. The conductor's wife, an obese woman wrapped in a floral print dress, bought from each of them. When the family had eaten, they threw the papers from the window into the right-of-way together with the coca bottles their father uncapped for them. "¡Magdalena!" the conductor roared. Beatriz smiled stoically. "Two hours to go still to Nogales," she remarked. The train made a grumbling halt, and the inspector, turning to look from the window, instantly recognized the church rising above the white adobe houses canopied by shade trees along the familiar dirt streets.

Beyond Imuris the ocotillo, still in brilliant flower, gave way to coppery live oak. Here the wrinkled brown mountains too were familiar, like the green irrigated meadows, the arroyos filled with trash and car bodies, the cottonwood groves, and the orange-and-blue Pemex stations, all of which things inspired in the inspector something like nostalgia. He caught the conductor's eldest daughter staring at him and smiled at her before she could avert her face. "¿Como se llama?"

The girl giggled and looked away. "Rosa."

116

"¿Habla inglés?"

"¡No!" She emphasized the negative with a shake of her head and looked to her mother as if to learn whether conversing with the stranger were acceptable behavior or not, but the woman sat engorging a heavily sugared pastry and paid her no attention.

The inspector, who had drunk three cups of coffee on top of the wine he had consumed at lunch, felt the need to walk back to the vestibule where elderly campesinos in cowboy hats stood crowded with young couples embracing with their arms around each other's necks. He entered one of the two facing compartments and relieved himself on a pile of paper napkins printed over with lipstick that clogged the toilet. On his way out he collided with a pretty girl entering. In his embarrassment at having mistaken DAMAS for CABALLEROS, the inspector turned the wrong way in the vestibule and pushed past several of the amorous couples before he felt a wind in his face and, looking forward, saw that he had come to the steel apron between the cars. Here the campesinos stood smoking, among them a tall figure with whiskers surmounted by a ruined sombrero hat. "Are you feeling ill?" Beatriz asked him when he had returned to his seat. "You look white as a ghost, almost as if you were about to faint. Why don't you go stand at the end of the car and get some fresh air?"

The inspector said he was feeling all right, and Beatriz looked at her watch. "Less than an hour now," she encouraged him. "You'll have quite an adventure to tell about when you get home, won't you?"

He sat miserably on the armrest and stared at his clasped hands hanging between his knees. A man wearing the uniform of the Ferrocarriles Nacionales came along selling Tecate, and the inspector bought two beers from him. When Beatriz declined the second, he drank that too. "You must have been thirsty," she remarked. Rosa from boredom tried to get him to speak to her again, but the inspector was hardly agreeable. The train, making no further stops, barreled steadily northward while the conductor snored beside the green trunk, his chin supported by the rise of his paunch and his cap pulled over his eyes. Clasping his hands tighter still, the inspector thought of the station at Nogales, its crowds and police-

117

men and taxis to the border crossing. Aboard the train he had nothing to fear, surrounded by his fellow passengers and protected by the railroad employees. Someone knocked against his leg and stood painfully on his foot. "Permiso," the familiar contemptuous voice said as the inspector, looking up, received a short impersonal stare in return. The expatriate wore a light windbreaker beneath which the inspector's trained eye perceived the bulge of a holstered revolver under the left armpit. Blood banged in his ears as the expatriate pushed his way forward to the front of the car and turned round suddenly as if prepared to make an announcement. The inspector turned too and saw, at the opposite end of the coach, Alberto standing in the vestibule with his legs spread against the motion of the train and a hand thrust into the front of his blouse. In the dusty road beside the tracks the Chrysler ran beside the train, drawing behind itself a spiralling cone of dust.

The inspector had his deer-horn knife out in the same instant that the expatriate took hold of the emergency-stop cord and pulled on it. With his left hand he seized the conductor's shoulder across the seat back and shook him. In his extreme excitement he had lost the little Spanish it had taken nearly a quarter of a century to acquire, and he had difficulty now communicating his message to the drowsy man. When the conductor at last understood what was happening he began to bellow and wave his fat arms at the expatriate, who continued to jerk on the cord as the train charged ahead with unslackened speed. "Do you see that man trying to stop the train?" Beatriz asked. "They have holdups along the line all the time now. I'm very glad I haven't my good jewelry with me."

While the conductor stood roaring beside his trunk several campesinos rose from the crates on which they had been sitting and moved warily upon the expatriate, who drew his revolver and flourished it at them. Alberto too had his gun drawn, but he did not wave it, and no one but the inspector paid him any attention. The expatriate gave a final desperate pull on the cord, then vanished into the vestibule pursued by the campesinos and the conductor's threats. Simultaneously, Alberto retreated onto the platform at the opposite end of the car. A shout went up from in front, and the inspector, standing with the rest of the delighted passengers, saw

118

the expatriate, bareheaded, somersaulting down the embankment over trash and broken bottles and Jesús swerving the Chrysler into the shoulder of the road to pick him up.

"Suppose we'd had to stop for another train waiting on the track ahead?" Beatriz demanded. "At forty miles an hour everyone would have been killed. It really *is* a national disgrace, you know. Nothing in Mexico ever works."

PART THREE

"¡Olé!" The crowd roared as Pepe Ramos, kneeling in the sand of the arena with his slippered feet extended neatly behind himself, passed the bull on their first encounter with each other. "That is thrilling to watch," Beatriz Kattán-Ibarra remarked, "but it is the bravado of a very young man. Pepe will not live to kill many bulls if he insists on taking chances so early in the fight with an animal whose reactions he has not had time to study yet."

From their seats directly behind the barrera on the shady side of the ring Beatriz and the inspector watched the first corrida of the season in the company of five or six thousand spectators dressed in their Easter finery and drinking beer from paper cups as they remonstrated uproariously with el Presidente each time he awarded an ear or two ears or no ear at all. Earlier in the day the two of them had attended Mass together, the inspector sitting rigid with discomfort and embarrassment on the hard wooden bench while Beatriz knelt to pray and he deposited what remained of Father Velázquez's money in the black linen bag presented to him at the end of a wooden pole by the usher. Afterward they'd eaten a large luncheon in a handsome restaurant above a shopping arcade crowded with the cream of Nogales society, local politicians, and TV newsmen hoisting cameras on their shoulders. Following the meal, the two of them had spent the remaining hours before the fight drinking wine under an umbrella at a café out front of the bull ring and watching the people arrive, as behind the barred gates a band played pasos dobles and the picadores walked out their horses. "What if I get sick?" the inspector had asked, but Beatriz reassured him. "You won't be sick," she said. "The bull-fight is one of the few institutions in Mexico that hasn't anything sickening about it. The meaning of the bullfight is that death is not, after all, the worst thing in life, nor the most degrading."

Already he had watched five of the six bulls killed without feeling sickness or even squeamishness. He had understood that the episodes involving the horses were horrifying, but these horses were padded along their right flanks and the only one of them to be overset by a bull had struggled to its feet uninjured after several seconds. By the time the picador rode out to stick the third bull the inspector was booing and jeering him along with the rest of the crowd. The bright blood pumped from the morillo and ran in sheets over the glossy shoulders, and then the banderilleros came forward, racing at an oblique angle across the charging bull's path and springing to plant the banderillas above the shoulder blades. With his second bull Pepe Ramos placed his own banderillas, for which he received a great ovation.

Beatriz explained how Pepe Ramos was doing very well with this bull, working dangerously close in his pases naturales and veronicas but always with ease and exquisite control. At last he asked permission from the President to kill the bull. As Pepe Ramos raised the sword to the level of his shoulder, the inspector found himself from his position directly behind the torero sighting with him along the down-curved filament of steel to the vital place high between the shoulders. With the speed of a striking snake Ramos went directly in above the lowered horns. The sword, striking bone instead of the canopy of hide, sprang from his hand and fell end over end into the sand. While the bull continued to stand with what to the inspector seemed uncalled-for patience, Ramos retrieved the sword and positioned himself once more in front of the bull with his sword arm extended. The second stroke also failed to reach the heart, the sword penetrating only halfway to the guard and easing farther from the wound with each of the bull's heaving breaths.

When Pepe Ramos reached to pluck the sword from between the bloody shoulders the bull knocked him down and stood astride him, striking at the prone figure with its right horn. Ramos's men ran at the bull flapping their capes and shouting, but it refused to be lured away from the man lying motionless on his face in the sand. The inspector shut his eyes as tightly as he could. When he opened them he saw that Pepe Ramos was out from under the bull and on his feet again, once more with the killing sword in hand as boos echoed from around the ring and the blue-and-white striped pillows rained down from the tendidos. Once again Ramos faced the mortally wounded bull whose bellowing nearly covered the angry roar of the crowd. This time the sword sank to the guard between the shoulder blades as the bull, vomiting gouts of purple blood, sank to its knees and rolled onto its back with all four legs in the air under a continuing shower of pillows. "Did you notice how the right horn was atypically curved?" Beatriz asked as they were leaving the ring. "If that had been a normal horn, they would be laying Pepe out on the cooling board this very moment. Do you mind taking a minute to say hello to the young man? His father was a close friend of my late husband's."

Pepe Ramos stood with his wife and small son under the concrete flare of the stadium surrounded by pressmen and radio broadcasters wanting to interview him. He was a tall slim man with wavy black hair and sharp good looks, still wearing his elegant brocaded suit covered now with the dried blood of his dead opponent. He listened attentively to the questions that were put to him and answered intently and fluently and with much charm, turning aside implied criticisms with a smile and dropping his eyes modestly when he was complimented.

Beatriz approached him with the inspector following at her heels and, sweeping the reporters aside, threw her arms about the torero's neck. Then she embraced Señora Ramos and finally the little boy whom she knelt to embrace, placing his chin on her shoulder and his cheek against her own. The inspector, standing behind her, found himself looking into a pair of soft round eyes that widened as they stared back at him in curiosity first, then in growing alarm. There was something, the inspector felt, uncomfortably familiar about those eyes. Suddenly the small brown face contorted itself, and a round pink mouth opened wide. "¡Papá!" the little boy cried. "¡Ése es él! ¡El Diablo! ¡El Diablo! ¡Papá! ¡Papá! ¡Mira!"

The inspector looked, but this time there was no bougainvillea bush in which to hide.

Beyond the ring vendors hawked banderillas to the departing crowd, and the inspector just avoided having his pocket picked in a pickpocket scam. Beatriz hired a cab from the cab line on the boulevard and gave her address to the driver, who drove at high speed through red lights, past stop signs, and into streets marked NO EN-TRAR while a large black-and-white die suspended from the rearview mirror swung wildly. Her house was a low white construction surrounded by an expansive lawn shaded by palm and orange trees and enclosed by a tall iron fence in the city's best neighborhood. After a short altercation with the driver Beatriz paid the man half the sum he demanded and shut the door on his vigorous protest.

A sprinkler system cast slow precise veils of water toward them as they crossed the lawn, the droplets falling just short of the cement path. The glare of the evening sun on the exterior walls forced the inspector to squint, but inside the house was blue shadow and the coolness of a desert evening. Beatriz went to her bedroom without switching on the lights, while in the guest room the inspector gathered his few things in the overnight bag she had lent him and smoothed the bedclothes he had hastily made up that morning. Then, taking the bag with him, he returned to the sitting room, where he sat to wait in the deepening twilight.

She had furnished the house in a careful blending of modern and antique Spanish furniture with Indian pieces and designs. A row of ceramic trees of the kind familiar to him from Father Velázquez's rectory stood in order of ascending size along one wall. The inspector observed these, idly at first. Then he turned on a table lamp for a better look at the strange efflorations painted in lurid colors and crowded with birds, butterflies, and human figures. Clearly the work of primitive artists, they were entirely unselfconscious in their primitivism, their vulgarity merely a simple assertion of the force of nature and of human life itself. "What are those tree things?" the inspector asked as Beatriz entered the room wearing a turquoise blouse above white slacks and smoothing her rich copper hair.

"They are called Trees of Life. From the Tree of the Knowledge of Good and Evil. They are the symbol of Mexico. Indians in the south make them. They are lovely, don't you think?"

"I don't know." It occurred to him now that he'd passed one of the things through customs every once in a while.

"Take one home with you," she offered. "Take any one you like, as a souvenir of Mexico."

The inspector hesitated between the smallest and most gaudy tree and the next in size, which was more subdued. Finally he chose the larger one, and Beatriz brought a shopping bag for him to carry it in. Then they went together to the garage for the car.

Beyond Beatriz's neighborhood the narrow streets were sour with putrefying garbage and standing water behind clogged drains. Though tourists still crowded the bazaars and restaurants, the city had an air of exhaustion following the Easter fiesta. Behind the Port of Entry, a double line of American cars and recreational vehicles headed home from Guaymas and San Carlos extended for a good half-mile. Beatriz sighed. "I can walk it from here," the inspector offered.

"But you have all that way to go on the other side."

"It isn't that far, really."

"Let's sit a few minutes and see how fast the line moves," Beatriz suggested.

She found a classical-music station on the radio, and they listened to Bach and Pergolesi being broadcast from Tucson while the traffic crept forward in a haze of stinking exhaust. When a newsboy stopped beside the car the inspector took his last coin from his pocket and bought a paper with it. "Do you know Spanish well enough to read the newspaper?" Beatriz asked in surprise.

"Not really. I forgot I'm in Mexico. Do you want me to get out and walk now?"

"Suppose we wait five more minutes and see if it goes any faster."

"It won't. I've been watching it for thirty years."

He read the headline, which appeared to announce the result of a gubernatorial election, and turned over the pages which were

127

filled mostly by photographs. There were also a comics page, one of crossword puzzles and horoscopes, and several of sports news. The inspector went through the paper from front to back and then back to front again. He was about to offer it to Beatriz when his attention was caught by a photograph of a woman's sprawled corpse under the headline SE ENCUENTRA CONTRABANDISTA MUERTA A TIROS. The story, which was datelined Bavispe, had to do with the discovery of the partially decomposed body of a woman found shot to death beside a road in the Sierra de la Madre, apparently the victim of drug smugglers. Rendered anonymous by the shapeless clothing of the Mexican poor, the body rested on its side, the face hidden by shadow and by the right arm covering the head. The inspector studied the photograph for some time and finally lifted it to his eye, at which remove the image was no more than a formless collocation of black points on a white background. "Is it something interesting?" Beatriz inquired.

The inspector shook his head. He folded the tabloid and laid it gently on the seat between them. "I'm going to walk now," he said.

"Perhaps you'd better, if you expect to make it home tonight."

He opened the door and stepped out into the street, holding the ceramic tree in its paper bag. "Thank you so much for everything."

"Am I going to see you again?"

"I don't know. Wouldn't you be bored?"

"Why should I be bored?"

"I've been told I'm boring."

"Not to me. I'm proud of you for all the dangers and adventures you've been through."

"What time did you want to come across to go shopping tomorrow?"

"Noonish, I think."

"Then I'll see you at noon at the Americana. I owe you lunch, remember."

"Until tomorrow then. Don't I even get a kiss?"

They embraced through the open window as the traffic started to edge forward and the driver of the car behind sounded his horn.

The inspector set out carrying his bag in the direction of the Port of Entry, along the line of sedans and Winnebagos enclosing suffering impatient faces sealed in chill denatured air. He had gone two thirds of the distance when he realized that he had with him something to declare and no money to pay the duty with. He stopped, set the bag on the asphalt between his knees, and considered what to do.

The ceramic tree perhaps had a value below the duty-free limit, or perhaps much above it. The inspector had no idea of its market worth. It occurred to him to deposit the statue with the customs station and return later with the money to redeem it. If he were truly fortunate, a former colleague would be on duty and would pass him through on his honor with the tree. In either case he must get on the pedestrian line and stand for an hour or longer on the hard pavement breathing noxious fumes. The inspector thought of home, of a hot bath, a cold beer, of cool sheets over his own bed. He took up the bag again and walked rapidly across the square and into a quiet side street empty of tourists and beggars alike.

Cracked spittle-slick sidewalks led him past closed shops and eateries to the foot of a steep hill scarred by gravel slides and littered with garbage and the remains of avalanched shacks, where the street made a right-angle turn around a cantina from which rough voices and the blare of corridos sounded through barred windows. Three blocks ahead the chain-link fence that was the international border glistened in the dusk with an almost pearly light. Hastening toward it, the inspector found himself one of many figures converging silently upon a small crowd gathered around a man-sized hole cut from a section of steel mesh.

Most were young men, but there were also among them women with children and even a few elderly people. The inspector stood waiting his turn with them, jostled by tensed eager bodies as, one by one, they squeezed through the hole onto American soil and scattered in the growing dark. When the inspector's turn came he stepped swiftly, holding the paper bag carefully ahead of himself, and made off confidently with his smuggled treasure in the direction of home.

ABOUT THE AUTHOR

Chilton Williamson, Jr., was formerly history editor for St. Martin's Press and literary editor for *National Review*. For the past 19 years, he has been senior editor for books for *Chronicles: A Magazine of American Culture*. Born in New York City, he was raised in Manhattan and on the family farm in South Windham, Vermont. Since 1979, he has lived in Wyoming, except for two years spent in Las Cruces, New Mexico. Besides *Mexico Way*, Williamson is the author of two published novels and four works of nonfiction. With his wife, Maureen McCaffrey Williamson, he lives in Laramie, Wyoming.

Printed in the United States
123618LV00002B/159/P

9 780972 061681